"Trust me,"

Colin said.

"Trust you? How can I? I saw the way you looked at that newspaper. You have some crazy idea of solving your grandfather's murder. That's what this is all about, isn't it?"

"I don't know what you mean."

"Don't bother to deny it." Della met his gaze squarely as she moved out of his arms. "I recognize a man with a purpose when I see one."

"I have to know what kind of man Shawn Delaney was. Why he was murdered. If I understand, perhaps I can lay some demons to rest."

"Or be killed yourself."

He gave a dismissing wave of his hand. "Not possible. I didn't live in my great-grandfather's day."

With a tremor in her voice, she corrected him. "You do now."

Dear Reader,

We've got six more exciting books for you this month, so I won't waste any time before telling you all about them. First off, we've got *Caitlin's Guardian Angel*. This book represents a real milestone; it's the *fiftieth* Silhouette title by one of your favorite authors: Marie Ferrarella. It's also our Heartbreaker title for the month, and hero Graham Redhawk certainly lives up to his billing. You'll find yourself rooting for him in his custody battle for the adopted son he adores—and in his love for Caitlin Cassidy, the one woman he's never forgotten.

By now you know that our Spellbound titles are always a little bit different, and Lee Karr's *A Twist in Time* is no exception. Join forces with the hero and heroine as they journey into the past to investigate a murder whose solution is the only way to guarantee their own future. Laura Parker begins a new miniseries, Rogues' Gallery, with *Tiger in the Rain*. Years ago, Michaela Bellegarde brought Guy Matherson the best luck of his life. Now he's forced to turn to her once again— but this time, danger is on his trail. Leann Harris returns with *Trouble in Texas,* the story of a woman doctor "stranded" in a small Texas town. Love with the local sheriff is definitely the cure for what ails her, but, as so often happens, the road to recovery is not an easy one. Historical author Jessica Douglass makes her contemporary debut with *Montana Rogue,* a story of kidnapping, rescue—and romance. Don't miss it! Finally, welcome new author Amelia Autin. In *Gideon's Bride* she tells the story of a mail-order marriage threatened by the bride's deep, dark secret.

So sit back and enjoy all six of this month's Intimate Moments titles, then come back next month, when we bring you six more compellingly romantic books by some of the best writers in the business.

Yours,

Leslie Wainger
Senior Editor and Editorial Coordinator

Please address questions and book requests to:
Silhouette Reader Service
U.S.: 3010 Walden Ave., P.O. Box 1325, Buffalo, NY 14269
Canadian: P.O. Box 609, Fort Erie, Ont. L2A 5X3

MVFOL

*G*ET ALL THIS *F*REE

WITH JUST ONE PROOF OF PURCHASE:

$50 VALUE

◆ **Hotel Discounts** up to 60% at home and abroad ◆ **Travel Service -** Guaranteed lowest published airfares plus 5% cash back on tickets ◆ **$25 Travel Voucher** ◆ **Sensuous Petite Parfumerie** collection ◆ **Insider Tips Letter** with sneak previews of upcoming books

*Y*ou'll get a FREE personal card, too. It's your passport to all these benefits– and to even more great gifts & benefits to come!

There's no club to join. No purchase commitment. No obligation.

SIM-PP5A

Enrollment Form

☐ *Yes!* I WANT TO BE A *Privileged Woman*.

Enclosed is one *PAGES & PRIVILEGES*™ Proof of Purchase from any Harlequin or Silhouette book currently for sale in stores (Proofs of Purchase are found on the back pages of books) and the store cash register receipt. Please enroll me in *PAGES & PRIVILEGES*™. Send my Welcome Kit and FREE Gifts — and activate my FREE benefits — immediately.

More great gifts and benefits to come.

► DETACH HERE AND MAIL TODAY! ►

NAME (please print)

ADDRESS   APT. NO

CITY   STATE   ZIP/POSTAL CODE

PROOF OF PURCHASE ONLY

NO CLUB!
NO COMMITMENT!
Just one purchase brings you great Free Gifts and Benefits!

Please allow 6-8 weeks for delivery. Quantities are limited. We reserve the right to substitute items. Enroll before October 31, 1995 and receive one full year of benefits.

Name of store where this book was purchased_____

Date of purchase_____

Type of store:

☐ Bookstore   ☐ Supermarket   ☐ Drugstore
☐ Dept. or discount store (e.g. K-Mart or Walmart)
☐ Other (specify)_____

Which Harlequin or Silhouette series do you usually read?

_____

Complete and mail with one Proof of Purchase and store receipt to:

U.S.: *PAGES & PRIVILEGES*™, P.O. Box 1960, Danbury, CT 06813-1960

Canada: *PAGES & PRIVILEGES*™, 49-6A The Donway West, P.O. 813, North York, ON M3C 2E8

SIM-PP5B

A TWIST IN TIME

LEE KARR

Silhouette®

INTIMATE™MOMENTS®

Published by Silhouette Books

America's Publisher of Contemporary Romance

SILHOUETTE BOOKS

ISBN 0-373-07662-2

A TWIST IN TIME

Copyright © 1995 by Leona Karr

Printed in U.S.A.

Books by Lee Karr

Silhouette Intimate Moments

A Twist in Time #662

Silhouette Shadows

Stranger in the Mist #3
Footsteps in the Night #15

LEE KARR

is a multipublished author of Gothic romances and suspense novels. An avid reader, her favorite books have always been those that send her heart pounding and bring a dry lump of fear into her throat. When she isn't writing and reading, she enjoys visiting her four children and traveling into the Colorado mountains.

Chapter 1

Della Arnell crossed her arms and shivered as she looked out the window of the old hotel she'd recently bought for renovation. Despite an expensive new heating system, a chill remained in the high-ceilinged rooms and lobby of the historic building. In the darkness of rain and shadow, streetlights stood like lonely sentinels along the sidewalks of lower downtown Denver.

Staring out, she tried to focus beyond the streams of water assaulting the windowpane. She could barely make out a vacant lot and an old warehouse across the street. Most of the buildings on the famous "Row," Denver's 1880s red-light district, were being torn down or renovated. In the steady downpour of black rain, the street was without any sign of life. She was about to turn away, when a hand and face suddenly pressed against the glass at eye level. She cried out and jerked back.

The shadowy face disappeared and in the next moment there was pounding on the front door. "Let me in, Della."

Above the noise of the rain, she recognized Colin Delaney's voice. Relieved and angry at the same time, she opened the door to the dark-haired Irishman. "What on earth do you think you're doing, scaring me like that?" she railed.

"I didn't mean to frighten you." Thick black eyebrows and eyelashes dripped water as he squinted at her. "Sorry," he said gruffly as he brushed back the hair waving darkly around his face.

She would have preferred that a smile accompany his apology, but in the few weeks she'd known Colin, his strong Celtic features rarely softened into casual smiles. His rugged good looks had intrigued her when they first met, but something about his guarded nature made her uneasy. She wondered why he was paying her a visit on such a stormy night.

A flash of lightning forked across the night sky, followed by a loud clap of vibrating thunder. All at once, the chilled air in the hotel snapped with electricity, as if Colin had brought the storm in with him. As he stood there, looming over her, his face in shadow, Della wished he hadn't come. She was suddenly uneasy for the first time since she had moved into the empty three-story hotel. During the day, the place was filled with workmen doing the renovations, but at night she was alone—and vulnerable.

She gave herself a mental shake. Colin Delaney had sold her this hotel, which had been in his family for four generations, and she was satisfied that the investment would pay off now that the new Rockies baseball field was completed. All of her dealings with Colin had been straightforward and businesslike. Why was she uneasy about this visit?

"Did you walk from your office in this downpour?" she asked, trying to make some sense out of his showing up in the midst of lightning and thunder. As he took off his lightweight raincoat, she saw that the soft navy slacks and a light summer pullover damply accented his hard physique.

"I suppose I could have called, but I wanted to talk to you face-to-face," he admitted.

She was puzzled. From the first time she'd met Colin Delaney, she'd felt peculiarly off stride around him and found his strong masculine energy disconcerting. She knew he was a bachelor with no immediate family, and as far as she knew, no serious relationships at the moment. But he gave every indication of knowing his way around women. As much as she may have been tempted, their business relationship had never edged toward anything personal. Any romantic entanglement with a man like Colin Delaney would create the kind of emotional waves that Della had been trying to avoid. She wasn't prim or frigid, only cautious when it came to her love life. She'd always been able to control her emotions, and the few men who had briefly romanced her had never threatened the deep feelings she kept hidden and protected. She had to admit, however, that Colin challenged that protective detachment. She didn't like the way he could engage her emotions without even seeming to realize he was doing it. She felt her defenses go up. "I don't understand what could be so urgent to bring you out on a night like this."

"It's important," he said flatly.

A lot of property in the area had come down through the Delaney family to Colin. She knew that his investment company was turning a couple of old warehouses into loft apartments just a couple of blocks away. But he'd been very tight-lipped about the reasons he'd decided not to renovate the historic Denver Railroad Hotel himself.

"All right. Come back to my apartment," Della said. Their footsteps echoed on the wooden floor as she led the way down a short hall to the three rooms behind the hotel office, which she had turned into her private apartment. Blending the old with the new had been a challenge. She'd cleaned the brick fireplace, polished blackened copper fixtures to a bright glow, freshened the elaborate moldings adorning the walls and ceilings, and chosen wallpaper and window hangings that were harmonious with the ambience of the original building. She had filled the apartment with some nice pieces of old furniture from her aunt's home and had added a few things she'd found in the shops on Larimer Street.

Much to her surprise, Colin nodded his approval as his measuring gaze went around the living room. "I like it."

His open appreciation of what she'd accomplished in her apartment disarmed her. "Thank you," she said as a spurt of pleasure rushed through her.

"I think you've made a good investment."

She laughed. "I hope so. My Aunt Frances would be horrified to see what I've done with the inheritance she left me. She never gambled on anything speculative. Always put her money in solid investments. The idea of buying this place and spending so much money on renovations would have sent her into orbit. My aunt wasn't sentimental about anything. She was a hard-nosed businesswoman.''

''Like you?'' Was there a hint of a smile at the corner of those appealing masculine lips?

''I owe my aunt for whatever business sense I have,'' she admitted. ''She raised my sister and me from the time we were ten and twelve. My parents were killed by a drunken motorist who demolished our car. Somehow Brenda and I miraculously survived the crash.''

''I didn't know you had a sister.''

An ache Della thought she'd conquered stabbed her. ''I'm two years older. Brenda never adjusted to Aunt Frances's strict upbringing and ran away from home when she was sixteen. She broke my heart and was a great disappointment to my aunt.''

''And you tried to make up for it?''

''I suppose so,'' she said thoughtfully. ''Yes. I guess I've always been what you'd call an overachiever.'' She gave a light dismissive laugh and fixed her gray-green eyes on him. She realized she was glad he'd come. ''Would you like a cup of coffee?''

He studied her for a moment as if debating whether or not to accept her gesture of hospitality. Then he nodded.

''Be back in a minute.'' She quickly prepared a tray in the kitchenette, and when she returned he was sitting in a wing chair that had been her aunt's favorite. His arms rested on the padded curves of the chair and soft cushions cradled his firm body as he leaned back.

Even though he was in a relaxed position, she sensed in him a guarded inner shield. Flickering, leaping flames were reflected in his blue-black eyes as he stared pensively into the fire. As she stood beside him, she was aware of long legs, muscular arms and shapely hands that reeked of masculine sensuality.

She set the tray on the coffee table and handed him one of the steaming cups.

"Thank you." His appraising gaze traveled boldly from her honey blond head to her scuffed shoes.

She stifled an impulse to tuck in the wispy strands of hair that had slipped out of her French braid. Her faded jeans, blue-checked short-sleeved blouse and dirty canvas shoes showed the wear and tear of a day spent in the middle of sawed boards and paint cans. The fact that she looked a mess upset her more than she was willing to admit. He could have called ahead and given her a little warning, she thought ruefully, and then silently laughed at herself. This unexpected visit was not a social call. He'd had plenty of chances to ask her out and hadn't.

"Sugar? Cream?" she asked.

"Black."

"I hope it's strong enough," she said as she sat down in the middle of a couch opposite his chair. Why had he come to see her tonight, in the middle of a storm? she wondered again. She studied him over the rim of her cup and felt a stab of awareness. Why did she have the feeling that his visit was going to affect her in some momentous way? Her stomach muscles suddenly tightened.

His long fingers curled around the cup. A soft brush of black hair showed darkly on his tanned wrists.

When he leaned forward in his chair, she found she was holding her breath in anticipation.

"Tell me about it," he ordered.

"What?" She looked blank.

"This afternoon on the phone, you said you'd made an interesting discovery about the hotel. What did you find?"

"Oh, that!" She gave a relieved wave of her hand. Is that why he'd come? She had called him on a business matter and on impulse had told him she'd show him something interesting the next time he came around. "I didn't mean to sound all that mysterious." She smiled. "We didn't find a cache of buried gold under a floorboard, or anything like that."

He didn't return her smile. "What did you find?"

She took a moment to set down her coffee cup. Something in his manner was making her nervous. "A relic of the hotel's shady past, that's all."

"What?"

"A couple of workmen were shoring up the floor in the basement corner of the building and found a tunnel."

The chords in his neck tightened. "Are you sure?"

"At first, we thought it might be an old wine cellar, but it's a tunnel, all right... a very old one. One of the men took a few steps inside and said it probably runs under the street."

She waited for his response and when he remained silent, she prodded, "Did you know about it?"

A shadow passed over his eyes. "I thought it had been destroyed long ago," he said tautly.

She didn't like the look in his eyes or his tone of voice. Anger was there, and something else, some deep emotion she couldn't quite identify. Hatred? Suppressed violence? She was taken back by the sudden lines around his mouth.

"I guess I should have known. Evil never stays buried," he said.

"I don't understand."

"You don't have to understand," he told her. "Just fill the damn thing in!"

His sharp tone brought a flash of color to her cheeks. She'd already instructed the workmen to close up the passage when they had time but she wasn't about to say so to him. His autocratic manner rankled. She looked him steadily in the face, her jaw set as rigid as his. "This is *my* property now. I'll decide what to do with it."

A black cloud crossed his face, then he swore, got to his feet and stared down at her. For a moment, she thought he was going to jerk her to her feet. Instead, he turned his back to her and put his hands on the mantel. Leaning against it, he stared into the fire.

She was bewildered by his dramatic reaction to the discovery of an old tunnel that had been closed off for years. What importance could it have after all this time?

He stood looking at the fire for a long while. The loud cracking of falling logs was the only sound in the room. Then he gave a deep sigh and turned around. "I suppose I'd better explain as best I can."

The anguish in his tone touched her. She wanted to say something but no words would come. Tiny lines deepened around his eyes, and he surprised her by sitting beside her on the couch. His nearness only heightened the disturbing physical awareness pulsating through her. He leaned his dark head against the sofa cushion and stared at the ceiling.

"What is it? I don't understand why you're so upset."

"The Delaney family has quite a sordid past. And that tunnel is a part of it."

If he hadn't been so intense, she would have chided him about family skeletons. The muscles in his hard cheeks flickered with suppressed anger, but there were other emotions in his eyes, hurt and sadness. She didn't know what to make of him. When he began to speak, his voice was soft, as if the words came from far, far away.

"When this hotel was built in 1880 one of the vacant lots across the street had a brothel sitting on it. The infamous Maude Mullen's Pleasure House. The tunnel you found connected this hotel to that whorehouse." He stared at some unseen point in front of his haunted eyes. "That's where my great-grandfather was murdered. Stabbed to death on its doorstep."

She knew that her mouth had dropped open. No wonder the discovery of the tunnel had given him an emotional jolt, she thought. "I didn't realize that the tunnel was tied in with any personal history. I haven't read much about old-time Denver," she confessed. She'd been raised in New Mexico and had only been in Denver for a few years, working as bookkeeper for an oil company until she bought the hotel. There must be more to the story, thought Della, more than he's telling. Why should he be so emotional about a tragedy that happened over a hundred years ago? She waited for him to go on but he just stared with narrowed eyes as if watching a film roll by in his mind.

She was uneasy with his silence. "Why don't you tell me about it. I never heard of your great-grandfather or what happened to him."

His mouth tightened in a hard line. "My illustrious forefathers debauched the Delaney name in great fashion. There's speculation that my great-grandfather, Shawn Delaney, ran all the illegal activities in Denver's early red-light strip and was murdered by someone who wanted to take over. Others claimed that a jealous lady of the night stabbed him to death." There was a grim edge to his voice. "A true Delaney. And he passed along his legacy."

"What legacy is that?"

"My mother called it the devil's spawn."

The devil's spawn. She stared at his ashen face. "Do you believe in such things?"

"I only know that the Delaney men passed on their dark genes," he said bitterly. "My grandfather, Shawn's son, grew up to be a ruthless slumlord, heartless and selfish, exploiting the run-down Market Street properties without ever putting one cent back into them. Everything touched by the Delaneys had the smell of decay and decadence."

"Were you close to him . . . your grandfather?"

"Hell, no. He wasn't close to anyone. Everyone said he was Shawn Delaney all over again, but he didn't get himself killed. He lived to be nearly ninety. His only son, my father, grew up to be a bastard in true Delaney fashion. He made life hell for my mother and drank himself to death before he was twenty-five."

"And you inherited all the Market Street property from your grandfather?"

He nodded. "I decided to sell most of it. I thought I could lay an ugly past to rest—but it just won't stay buried. Why did that blasted tunnel have to come to light? It's as if the ghost of Shawn Delaney just won't let go."

His talk of ghosts gave her a creepy feeling. She could hear wind and rain pounding the old building, and the tempo of lightning and thunder had increased. Once again, she felt a harmony between Colin's dark glower and the raging storm.

Maybe I shouldn't have bought property in this part of Denver. Maybe no matter how she painted and remodeled, Della thought, the hotel would remain the same depraved place as when a tunnel had connected it to a fancy bordello. Maybe the area's colored past would never be changed, either.

As if reading her thoughts, Colin said, "This was a wild part of Denver in the late 1880s. Variety halls, saloons, gambling houses, cribs, racy madams running houses of ill repute... you name it. Drugs. Gambling. Drinking. And hapless young women selling themselves."

Della's lips tightened. Young women plying their favors for money struck too close to home. As a runaway, her sister, Brenda, had taken up with men who paid her bills. In the end, she had thrown her life away on men and drugs.

Colin watched her face. "I should have torn down the blasted hotel instead of selling it to anybody."

"Don't be foolish." Her practical nature overrode her fantasies. "I came to you, remember? Property in this part of town was attracting a lot of investors and I knew that if I didn't buy it, somebody else would.

What's past is past!" she added more firmly than she felt at the moment.

"Not when it intrudes upon the present."

"Don't let it intrude," she answered bluntly.

"I wish it were as simple as that. I sold the hotel to you because I thought that you were the one who could give it a new life ... a different karma. But it's no use. Some places are like sinkholes, no matter how you try to cover them up, they suck the innocent in."

"I don't believe that finding an old tunnel changes anything about my hotel and its future. Maybe its history is sordid and ugly, but what happened over a hundred years ago is only a curiosity as far as I'm concerned."

A shaft of shadow crossed his face. "I hope to God you're right. I wouldn't want you to be drawn into any of the black machinations I've fought all my life." A fearsome pain crossed his eyes and a dark strangeness put his whole face in shadows. She wasn't afraid of him, but his presence completely unnerved her.

He must have felt her withdrawal. "I'm sorry. I can't expect you to understand." He turned away and said abruptly, "I'd better be going."

"Wait." She stood up and caught his arm. "I want to understand."

"No, don't try. I was wrong to come." He walked toward the hall.

"I'll see you out," she said quickly.

When they reached the front door, the force of the storm was evident again through the windowpane. A quickening wind swept down the street and a fresh onslaught of rain beat against the windows.

"It's raining harder than before," Della said.

Colin looked out the door and nodded. Then he unexpectedly reached over and took her hand. His touch was surprisingly gentle and warm, and at the same time firm and engulfing. A spiral of heat radiated through her at the contact.

"I didn't mean to involve you," he said quietly. "I wasn't thinking . . . or I wouldn't have come."

"It's all right. I'm sorry I was so insensitive about the tunnel. I didn't know anything about Shawn Delaney."

His hand tightened on hers and his body grew rigid. "My mother always said she couldn't tell our pictures apart . . . that I was his evil soul incarnate."

Della was horrified. "When did she tell you that?"

"The day before she killed herself."

He dropped her hand and turned swiftly toward the door. He jerked it open, and bent his head against the attack of wind and rain. The next minute he was gone, swallowed up in sheets of gray rain.

Della locked the door behind him and hugged herself as she stared out into the watery bedlam. Her thoughts reeled. What had Colin done to make his mother treat her son so horribly?

He radiated a hot, compelling passion that she feared could be devastating if he chose to unleash it upon a woman. Fervent, driven, obsessed, he attracted her on levels that went beyond common sense. She knew she was in danger of giving way to a physical, emotional and sexual attraction that could make her a stranger to herself. If she had any sense, she would keep a wide distance between herself and the handsome, brooding Colin Delaney.

She turned away from the front door and had taken only a few steps when she stopped short.

"What—"

She jerked her eyes upward. A high chandelier began to glow above her. The shadowy darkness disappeared before her startled gaze. She looked around the lobby in disbelief. A second earlier, the hotel had been dark and empty. Now the glitter of brass and dark red Victorian furnishings assaulted her vision.

Two young women stood at the bottom of the carpeted stairs. Dressed in low-cut satin gowns with draped bustles and ruffled swags, the painted ladies boldly lifted their satin skirts to mount the stairs. The harlots tossed their feathered, high-piled hair and disappeared into the shadows of the second-floor landing.

Della stared after them, unable to move. *I'm hallucinating. I have to be!*

Chapter 2

Della's breath was short and her heartbeat rapid. She was frightened and yet curious. She'd never closed her mind to new experiences and even as a warning went off in her head, she moved slowly to the bottom of the stairs. Putting a shaky hand on the newel post, she stared up the old staircase. There was no sign of the ghostly figures that had been there a moment before. Cautiously, she mounted one step, then another until she reached the first landing. After turning on a wall light, she looked down the hall in both directions.

Empty. Workmen's clutter was everywhere—lumber, sawhorses, boxes, sacks of plaster, cans of paint. Everywhere was the same mess she'd left earlier in the day.

She walked to the steps leading to the third floor and stared upward. She couldn't hear anything in the echoing darkness except the clatter of rain upon the roof. She swallowed a hard lump in her throat. The hotel was as it had always been.

She turned around and slowly went downstairs to the lobby. A wash of relief swept over her when she saw it was again in shadow, except for the night-light at the hotel entrance. The old chandelier was once again lost in the darkness of the vaulted ceiling. Everything was exactly as it had been before the weird impression of light and ghostly women.

Della's forehead beaded with nervous sweat as she looked around the lobby and up the empty staircase. How could her senses have fooled her so completely? She brushed a hand across her eyes and suddenly a swish of cold air hit her face, blowing her blond hair back from her face.

She cried out and turned to flee. For an instant, she saw the silhouette of a man reflected in the windowpane. Colin? In the next instant, the impression was gone. A bleak light from a streetlamp illuminated the deserted street outside.

She fled down the hall to her apartment. Her fingers trembled as she shut the door on the rest of the unoccupied hotel and leaned against it. Her heart hammered in her chest. Her breath caught. Her eyes went to the wing chair, which still held the impression of Colin's body. Could his obsession with the past have affected her more than she realized. Yes, that must be it. His emotional reaction to the discovery of the tunnel and his talk about Shawn Delaney's murder must have planted subliminal images in her mind. He had made the hotel's past come alive and she had momentarily lost touch with reality.

Angry with him and herself, she was tempted to call him and tell him what had happened. The impulse died quickly. She knew she wouldn't tell him. She wouldn't tell anybody. The whole thing was too bizarre.

She was tired. The problems of renovating the hotel were getting to her, and Colin's visit had unsettled her. She wasn't sure how she felt about him. He fascinated her, in a strange way. When he held her hand, she felt drawn to him in a way that mocked her usual cool demeanor toward attractive men. And when he'd talked about his mother, she'd been jolted by the force of raw emotion emanating from him. The hatred in his eyes when he'd talked about his great-grandfather had been so intense that even now she felt herself recoil from it. Surely he didn't believe anyone who had been dead over a hundred years could be responsible for tainting the heredity of all the Delaney men?

As she prepared for bed, Della was determined not to think about the odd experience in the lobby. Her vivid imagination had played a trick on her, that was all.

A few minutes later, on the edge of sleep, the vision came back so sharply and clearly, she could have described the old-fashioned gowns in detail: velvet green and red satin peplum overskirts pulled back into ruffled bustles that trailed down to the floor; low-cut necklines edged in silk flowers and gathered ecru lace; scalloped streamers and velvet-ribbon bows dotting full skirts and puffed sleeves. Even the lace gloves and glittering fans were clear in her memory. *I must have seen an old picture like that at some time,* she told herself. That was the only explanation that made sense.

* * *

The next couple of days were hectic and Della had little time or energy to think about anything but the renovation of the hotel. She solved one crisis only to be faced with another. The work proceeded at a snail's pace and the estimates of time and money were way off. She raised hell with the construction foreman and then called her banker who confirmed what she feared—her cash flow was edging toward the danger point.

"You better get those cost overruns under control," he told her.

She checked every invoice to make sure she wasn't being ripped off. Her investment was turning into a fiasco and confidence in her business judgment was waning. Della let the phone ring three times before she grabbed it impatiently and barked, "Hello."

"No need to ask you how your day's going," Colin said in his deep resonant voice. "You sound ready to eat bear."

"Bears, snails, rattlesnakes. Anything that moves."

"I guess this is a bad time to remind you about the civic development dinner. I was going to suggest that I stop by and we walk over to the restaurant together."

She ran an agitated hand through her mussed blond hair. "I'd forgotten about it. I don't think I'll be going."

"It's important that everyone pull together to make the area a financial success," he said in a reasonable tone that added to her irritation.

"I know that," she snapped. "Save your chamber of commerce speech for someone else." Then she instantly felt ashamed. She leaned back in her chair and threw down her pencil. "I'm sorry. It's just that...well, I wouldn't be very good company."

"You have to eat," he answered reasonably. "And I could round up a snail or two to put on your plate if that will make you happy."

She was surprised at his light tone. She could picture a slight smile on the edge of his lips. *Well, why not,* she thought. Maybe she just needed to share her problems with someone who would understand. Besides, she really wanted to see him again. He'd been in her thoughts more than she was willing to admit.

"Forget the snails, bears and rattlesnakes," she said. "Roast beef will do fine."

"Good. I'll pick you up about seven-thirty. The restaurant's only a few blocks away. If you don't mind walking...?"

"I don't mind. See you then." She hung up, surprised to find that their brief conversation had somehow restored her equilibrium. With new energy, she cleared off her desk and then left the office. She walked all over the hotel, checking on the work.

She was on the third floor talking to a painter, when a brush of cold air hit her face and she broke off in midsentence. At the same instant, she heard the sound of running water, and a woman's soft laugh came from a nearby room that had originally been a shared bath. When Della jerked open the door, she couldn't believe her eyes.

A voluptuous naked woman with red hair piled high on her head was taking a bath in the old claw-footed tub. She hummed contentedly and poured water over her face with cupped fleshy hands.

Della gave a choked cry.

"What's the matter, miss?" asked the small wizened man who was filling his paint tray a few steps away. Della pointed.

He walked over, looked into the bathroom and shrugged. "Just an old tub. Don't see nothing to get excited about."

"That's all you see? An old tub?" An arctic chill crept up her spine.

"Yep." He gave her a queer look and returned to his painting.

Della looked again. The old tub was empty and dry. And yet she was positive she could still hear humming and splashing water. Like someone caught in a nightmare, she turned and walked away. When she reached the stairwell, she looked back down the hall. The shadow of a man stood watching her, his stance frighteningly familiar. *Colin?*

She pressed her hands against her temples. *I've lost my mind.* Crazy people couldn't distinguish between reality and fantasy. *And neither can I.* The woman in the bathtub, the old-fashioned ladies wandering through the hall, the man in the shadows, they were all in her mind. No one else was aware of the invaders. No one else seemed to notice whiffs of cheap perfume overriding the paint smells. She was the only one aware of the ghosts who had taken over her hotel.

When Colin came to pick her up, he eyed the strained lines around her mouth and the dull glaze in her gray-green eyes. She was like a tight spring ready to pop, every muscle tense and rigid. Her soft appealing lips were taut. Her nervous hands smoothed the skirt of her simple white dress and tugged at a soft pink scarf looped in a puff at her neck. "You weren't kidding about having a bad day, were you?"

She opened her mouth as if to say something but then closed it and only nodded.

He was puzzled by her behavior. She'd always shown extreme self-direction and competence while handling the business end of buying the hotel and arranging for its renovation. More than once, he'd admired her direct, unemotional approach to problems. She was a rare combination of strength and feminine softness. From the first moment he'd met her, she'd intrigued him. Intelligent. Fascinating. And beautiful. The direct unblinking beauty of her large eyes haunted him. The proud lift of her chin made him want to cup her face in his hands and taste her sweet lips. He wanted her.

But he knew better than to bring any woman into his life. His mother had warned him that Delaney men brought only destruction to those foolish enough to fall in love with them. His heart constricted when he thought about Elena, his first love, who had drowned before his very eyes. God forgive him if he'd already betrayed Della Arnell by selling the hotel to her.

"If you really don't want to go...?" *I should have stayed away from her,* he thought when he saw her ashen face.

"No, it's all right. I have to get out of this place." She turned away abruptly and preceded him out the front door.

He silently swore. *It was the hotel. The blasted hotel.* The past was like a cancerous growth that would not go away.

They walked in silence. After a couple of blocks, Della was aware that Colin was striding beside her with a ferocity that did little to ease the tightness in her chest and stomach. Why had she agreed to go with him? Her lips quivered. *Desperation, that's why.* She hadn't wanted to be alone in the hotel—*alone with ghosts of the past.*

He stopped abruptly when they reached the restaurant. "I don't feel like going to any meeting." He put a hand on her elbow and guided her past the café. "I hope you don't mind."

"Not at all." She was relieved that he'd been perceptive enough to know that sitting in a room full of businesspeople, making polite remarks and trying to listen to a dinner speaker were more than she could handle.

She glanced at his profile and saw tight muscles flickering in his taut cheeks. Had her mood affected him so much that he was willing to forgo his civic duty? What was going on behind those deep-set eyes of his? His dedication to upgrading Market and Larimer streets was almost a religious passion, as if he felt compelled to single-handedly eradicate all evidence of the town's early red-light district. Once again she wondered if his obsession with the past could somehow be responsible for her terrifying fantasies. Had he mesmerized her in some way, so that she was seeing the hotel through a historical haze?

He caught her apprehensive look and pulled her to a stop. "What's the matter? You're looking at me as if I have horns sprouting from my forehead. Tell me what's going on."

She moistened her lips. *I'm going crazy. Old-fashioned ladies of the night are wandering around my hotel. I even found one taking a bath upstairs.* For a horrid moment, she wasn't sure whether or not she had spoken her thoughts aloud. When his expression remained the same, she knew that he was still waiting for an answer.

"I...I've been having bad dreams," she stammered. That was close enough. Dreams were accepted as a sane phenomenon and she couldn't tell him the truth. She couldn't tell anyone. She kept her eyes focused slightly to the right of his face so she wouldn't have to meet his eyes.

"What kind of dreams?"

"I...I don't remember," she lied.

His dark eyebrows narrowed over the bridge of his nose. "You don't remember?"

She pointed to an outdoor café across the street. "I need a drink."

They were waiting for the light to change when the sidewalk suddenly dipped beneath her feet. She gasped, wavered and grabbed Colin to steady herself. *What was happening?*

She could see Colin's lips moving but couldn't hear what he was saying. Everything around her was in flux. Panic-stricken, her eyes darted in every direction. The buildings, the people, the smells, the noise. Her ears roared with the sound of horses neighing and carriage wheels clattering over rough streets. She cried out and covered her ears with her hands.

"What's wrong?" she heard Colin ask.

She tried to jerk away from him as he pulled her against him, caught in a panicked impulse to flee, to hide, to escape from the assaulting sounds and sights that had no reality. "Let me go," she sobbed against his chest.

"It's all right, it's all right." He stroked her hair and put his lips against her moist forehead.

After a moment, the ground stabilized under her feet. With terror caught in her throat, Della gingerly raised her head from his chest. No horses, no wagons, no unfamiliar buildings. Cars roared by and the whirling blades of a helicopter sounded overhead. The stores, the people and the shops were just as they had been. Her strangled breath came in short gasps.

"Let's get that drink," he said. He kept a firm arm around her waist as he guided her across the street to the outdoor café, and eased her onto one of the chairs. "Scotch and water," he barked to a hovering waiter and held up two fingers. Then he sat down opposite her. "All right. Tell me what's going on."

"I guess I had some kind of... of a spell," she said lamely. She wanted to tell him what was happening to her but she couldn't reveal the unbelievable truth. *I see and hear things that aren't there. I think I'm going crazy.*

He frowned. "Your eyes were round with terror. Something frightened you." His intense blue eyes suddenly darkened to almost black. "Don't lie to me."

"Why should I lie to you?" she said with some of her normal spirit. "Please don't ask me to explain. I need time to sort things out. And I don't want to talk about it, all right?" How could she tell him what was happening to her when she didn't know, herself?

The waiter arrived with the drinks. She held her glass with trembling hands and gratefully let the fiery liquid ease down her throat. She kept her eyes lowered.

Colin's troubled gaze appraised her over the rim of his menu. "I recommend the black bean soup and Monte Carlo sandwich." She nodded and he ordered another drink with their food.

The surrounding laughter and easy chatter of other diners was reassuring. An early-evening crowd sauntered along the sidewalk in front of the café, and slowly the weird illusion of horses and wagons faded as if it had never happened. She began to relax.

When their order came, and she had eaten what little she could, Della glanced anxiously at Colin. What must he think of her? "I'm really sorry," she said. "I don't know what came over me."

"I want to know what happened." He leaned forward, offering his hand, but she didn't take it. Instead, she drew back in her chair. His mouth tightened and a muscle quivered in his cheek.

She could see that her rejection had offended him. But how could she explain that she was entertaining dangerous feelings about him that were too strong to deny. He was engaging her emotions on levels she had never felt before. If the truth were known, he scared her.

"I know about dreams...nightmares...unexplained visions," he said as if trying to encourage her confidence. "Don't be afraid. You can share them with me." The blue in his eyes deepened to a strange feathery black. "I'll understand."

She stared at him and suddenly her mouth went dry. *I'll understand.* The shadowy figure at the end of the hall and the outline at the rain-streaked door...both times the impressions had made her think of Colin. And now, on the street, he had been with her when the bizarre illusion had assaulted her. Her pulse began to pound in her temples. Her thoughts whirled. *Get hold of yourself.* She really *was* losing it. Trying to tie Colin in with the aberrations of her mind was utterly ridiculous. She felt herself coloring under his measuring stare.

"I knew ... I knew I was too tired to go out tonight," she stammered. "You should have gone to the dinner without me. It's still early. You can still make the meeting ..."

"Damn the meeting," he said gruffly. He quickly paid the bill and they left.

Silence built a wall between them on the way back to her hotel. When they reached the front door, he took the key from her trembling hands. Ignoring her pointed "Thanks ... goodbye," he followed her into the lobby.

Della sent a frantic look at the staircase. Empty. No painted ladies. No bright lights. Nothing. If she took him upstairs, there would be nothing to show him there, either. No harlots parading in and out of rooms in their gaudy satin dresses, no voluptuous redhead taking a bath in an old tub.

He stood behind her and she could feel the warmth of his breath on her neck. A sob caught in her throat and hot tears spilled into the corners of her eyes. He put his hands on her arms. Gently he eased her against his strong firm body. "Tell me. Whatever it is, we need to share it."

The last fiber of her resistance melted away. She took a tremulous deep breath. "I don't know what's happening to me. Tonight on the street . . . everything changed," she said in a strangled voice. "The buildings. The people. I heard horses and carriages." She turned to face him. "And in the hotel, I see women. Old-fashioned harlots. Painted faces, low-cut gaudy dresses, hair piled high on their heads. Wandering up and down the stairs. In the halls. Taking baths."

"Good God." His voice cracked.

"Nobody else sees them . . . only me. I don't know—" She broke off. Like an explosion, a raucous noise vibrating down the halls and ricocheting off the high ceilings shattered the silence of the empty hotel. A cacophony of laughter, tinny music and clinking glasses rose and fell in waves and vibrated through the echoing building.

"What the hell—" Colin swore.

"You hear it, too?" Suddenly, she wanted to laugh and cry at the same time. The bewildering onslaught of noise wasn't just in her mind. She wasn't alone.

Colin strode to the bottom of the stairs, listened and then shook his head. "It must be coming from somewhere at the back of the building." He grabbed her hand. "Come on. Let's find out what the hell is going on."

The racket grew louder as they reached a back entrance and the stone stairs descending into the basement.

"Oh, no!" Della shot an apprehensive look at Colin. She knew where their search would end. "The tunnel."

"Didn't you close the damn thing up?" He strode angrily down the stairs.

The basement was dank and drafty with a bare electric light hanging from the open-beam ceiling. At one end of the room, a crude opening yawned in the rock wall. Cold air swept out of the passage and Della hugged herself against the chill. The loud thumping of piano, laughter and singing created a deafening din.

"It's coming from the tunnel, all right," Colin said.

"But how can that be? There's only a vacant lot across the street."

Colin's eyes burned into hers. "Then none of this is happening. We're both hallucinating." His voice lowered to a growl. "Maybe *you* buy that but I don't. All my life, I've been shackled to the past. This is my great-grandfather's mean spirit calling to me."

In one frightening second Della knew that he was going to rush into the black tunnel.

"Go back upstairs," he ordered.

"No," she screamed, grabbing his hand and trying to pull him back.

He gave her a shove and turned toward the tunnel. In the next instant, he was gone. Della had not intended to follow him, but before she could move back from the opening, a blast of cold air sucked her forward.

"Colin!" she cried out, twisting and turning, unable to free herself from the propelling force driving her into the tunnel.

In the darkness of the passage, he reached out and grabbed her hand. A gale like the intense sucking force in a wind tunnel swept them both forward. Caught in a whipping, swirling hurricane, they clung to each other as they traveled through the passage.

A split second? An eternity? Della never knew. Flashes of bright lights. The brilliant hues of rampant flowers. Almost imperceptibly, the dank smell of the tunnel was replaced by a sweet floral perfume. A kaleidoscope of colors blinded her with stabbing intensity. The wind died and Della felt the ground beneath them level out.

They clung to each other. When they regained their balance and could see again, they were standing in the foyer of Maude's Pleasure House on Market Street, dressed in the fashions of the 1880s.

Chapter 3

The bordello blazed with lights. Fiddle and piano music, crescendos of laughter and the din of high-pitched voices floated out into a center hall from several arched doorways. Della's throat tightened and the palms of her hands beaded with hot sweat. The same kind of women she had seen wandering around her hotel paraded up and down the staircase on the arms of purposeful-looking men. They were not vague and shadowy figures but horribly real.

Even as Della fought against the reality that bombarded her senses, a plump woman in her forties with a homely face, sharp nose and double chins paused at the top of a center staircase. She rested one bejeweled hand on the polished banister and looked down at Colin and Della as if she could reduce them to dust with one wave of her gnarled hand.

Della stared in disbelief. Rounded hips and full breasts stretched the fabric of her low-cut gown. An elaborate twist of false red hair held in place on top of her head by feathers and jeweled pins added to her height. Her complexion was sallow even with rouge and powder and there was a hawklike sharpness to her gray eyes, cold and impaling. She had nostrils that flared and a mouth that showed large ugly teeth. Della wanted to turn and run but her legs wouldn't move.

The woman lifted the train of her deep blue taffeta gown, came down the steps and crossed a wide entrance hall to the foyer where they stood. The reek of cheap perfume touched Della's nostrils with familiarity.

"I'm Maude Mullen," she said in a guttural voice. "It's about time somebody answered my ad." She eyed Colin up and down like someone judging horseflesh. "The job is part-time handyman and bouncer. Pay is a dollar a day. Be on the job by ten in the morning and at the bar by seven in the evening, except on Sunday. You keep your hands off the merchandise. Got it? Well, do you want the job or not?"

Colin hesitated for a moment and then nodded. He didn't know what else to do. The woman had obviously mistaken him for someone else. He could use the precious time to figure out what in the hell was going on.

Maude turned her sharp calculating eyes on Della. "As for you. Not much to look at...too thin. But that don't matter. Vinetta Gray was with me for twenty years. Best damn bookkeeper I ever saw. Kept the cleanest set of books on Market Street. You do the same . . . or else—got me? Any juggling with the numbers, I'll know it. I don't tolerate liars or cheats." Her nostrils quivered and she set her painted lips in an ugly line. "If I find you've been less than honest with me, you'll wish you never set foot in this place."

Della opened her mouth but Colin put his hand on her elbow and gave it a warning squeeze. *Don't say anything.*

She wanted to argue with him. They were making a mistake, she was certain of it. Surely it would be better to tell this madam that they weren't the people she thought they were. Every minute they carried on the horrible charade, they could be sinking deeper and deeper into some incomprehensible horror. Della's chest was so tight, she couldn't breathe.

"Names?" Maude demanded.

"Colin...and Della," he answered evenly. His composed expression sent a prickling of fear down Della's back. Why was he acting as if this were some normal introduction instead of a hideous nightmare?

"You got last names?"

"It's Miss Arnell and Mr. Colin," he lied.

"All right, I'll give you two a try." The woman's stabbing glare shot from Colin to Della. "If you've got something to say, spill it now. I run the best house this side of St. Louis. Three drawing rooms, an evening buffet, beer at a dollar a draw and five dollars for a split of champagne. Eighteen rooms, and my share is half the take. The last two years, 1886 and '87, were pretty good. Too early to tell what '88 will be. The damn self-righteous citizens of Denver are on the warpath." Her sharp eyes went from Della to Colin. "You two sharing the sheets?"

"No," said Colin evenly. "We just ... arrived together."

"All right. You can have Vinetta's old room," she told Della. "And, Mr. Colin, get yourself a room at the boardinghouse next door. Just remember, if you two want to stay, you follow the rules of the house just like everybody else."

Della didn't want to stay. She wanted the bizarre illusion to end. Every ounce of her common sense rejected the unbelievable situation. They couldn't really be here ... caught in a malicious time warp that had sent them back over a hundred years. In a minute, the spell would be over. Everything would be back to normal.

Colin was saying something to the woman but Della didn't hear the words. Her mind refused to work. Immobilized from shock, she stared at the madam who was treating her like a newly hired bookkeeper. She wanted to laugh and had to clamp her mouth shut to keep the hysterical laughter at bay. She closed her eyes for a moment and prayed that when she opened them, everything would have returned to normal.

"You look puny to me, Della. I don't want some sickly gal on my hands." Maude glared at her. "I got a house to run. I need to know exactly how much money's coming in and going out on a nightly basis. I got plenty of expenses. The girls pay room and board but my grocery bill looks like I'm running the Brown Palace. I need a good bookkeeper." She scowled. "I'm not handing out any charity. You'll either do the job or you'll be out in the street on your scrawny behind. Understand?"

Della managed to nod.

Maude snorted. "Well, I'll know soon enough if you can add two and two." She gave a jerk of her head. "Come on back to my office, both of you. You can start work tomorrow."

Della held back. Her eyes widened in panic. *We can't stay here.*

Colin bent his dark head close to hers. "We have to play along until this whole thing makes some sense."

"And what if it never makes sense?" she protested in a desperate whisper. Was it possible? Transported back in time to the turn of the century? Set down in the middle of Denver's red-light district? "We have to go... before we get trapped."

His face shadowed. "We're already trapped."

The cold finality of his words shattered something deep within her. He was a stranger, dressed in a black double-breasted waistcoat and trousers, white shirt with a stiff white collar, a soft gray tie looped at the neck and even a gold pocket-watch chain stretched across his waist. It disarmed her to see that his dark handsome looks were in harmony with their surroundings as if born to them.

"We have to find the tunnel!" A new edge of panic made her voice sharp. She stared at him with a horrible feeling that he had become someone else. Someone she didn't know at all. Had he somehow engineered the time warp? Had he bolted back into the past because he belonged there? "How are we going to get out of this?"

"I don't know." Her safety weighed heavily on him. Desperation had drawn him into the tunnel, a desperation to be free of the past, but she was an innocent victim in these bizarre happenings. He had to protect her but he would be damned if he knew how. "You'll have to trust me."

Trust him?

"Are you two coming?" Maude asked impatiently as she turned around and saw them still standing in the foyer.

Colin searched Della's face and waited for her reluctant nod before he answered, "Yes, we're coming." He murmured to Della, "Try to pretend that everything's normal."

She wanted to laugh hysterically at the word *normal*. How could any situation be further from normal than this one? If they tried to convince the horrible Maude Mullen who they really were, she would probably have them hauled off to the nearest asylum. Della shuddered just thinking about the possibility. Asylums in the nineteenth century were hellholes. A whorehouse might not be a desirable choice for a roof over their heads, but at the moment it was the better option. Maybe Colin was right. Their situation was too precarious for them to admit anything about their true identities. She took a deep breath and murmured, "All right. I'll try to act...normal."

At that moment, two young women dressed in satin and rose-trimmed ballgowns went up the stairs in the company of two attentive middle-aged men. Della had the sensation that she had seen the women before...going up the staircase of her own hotel...but there was one difference. These women were flesh and blood. She could have reached out and touched their warm and breathing bodies. If they were only specters, then so was she, Della thought with new horror.

She touched the ecru lace collar at her neck and fingered the small bone buttons that ran down the front of her dark brown dress. Strange undergarments cinched her waist and lifted her breasts. Her brown shoes had narrow heels and laces like the old-fashioned look that had come back into style, and her hair was no longer loose but caught in a bun at the back of her head. If she was fantasizing, no detail in her dress had been overlooked by her imagination.

Colin kept a firm grip on her elbow as they walked down the hall. His mind raced. The tunnel led from the hotel, under the street to this brothel and somehow they had ended up on Maude's doorstep. If he located the opening of the tunnel, was there some way to reverse what had happened? Could he send Della back through the passage? God forgive him if he had somehow dragged her into the dark quagmire of his heritage.

As they walked down a center hall, Della glimpsed Victorian drawing rooms with ornate furniture covered in silk and damask. Richly dressed young women sat on ottomans or stood beside fashionably dressed men of all ages. A gaudy opulence radiated from gilded plaster designs embellishing the ceilings and walls of the rooms. In one of the rooms, couples were dancing to piano music. The men were all drinking and eating as if they were guests at an elaborate party. The combined sound of music, laughter and talking was deafening. Well, we found out where the noise was coming from, she thought with bitter irony.

"Let me do the talking," Colin cautioned as they followed Maude into her office. He gave Della a reassuring smile that didn't reach his eyes, but she was more than willing to let him take the lead, at least for now.

Maude's office was a spacious room that originally might have been intended to be a library, Della guessed. Bookcases lining two walls contained only a smattering of books, but the room was crowded with furniture, lamps, knickknacks, a huge horsehair sofa and matching chairs covered in leather. An elegant desk made of black walnut dominated the center of the room. A collector's dream, thought Della.

Maude motioned to a small, plain desk stacked with heavy ledgers that was placed against the back wall. "That's your desk, Della. Be at it by eight o'clock every morning but Sunday. I'll come downstairs between ten and eleven to go over the previous night's receipts."

Della wanted to sit down. Her legs felt too weak to hold her. Her knees threatened to buckle at any moment.

Maude waddled across the room and opened a door leading to a back hall. "Your room is past the kitchen, second door. The cook and housemaid have the other two rooms. I haven't moved Vinetta's things. We just buried her a week ago. You'll find things just as she left them."

Della's stomach took a sickening plunge. She didn't want to have anything to do with a dead woman's room, didn't want to be surrounded by Vinetta's personal belongings. She sent an anxious look at Colin, pleading with her eyes for him to say something.

"The back wing of the house is off limits to males," Maude snapped, having apparently intercepted the look they'd exchanged. "No danger of any of our

gentlemen guests mistaking you for one of our
'boarders.' Not that you'd have to worry," she added
quickly as she gave Della's slenderness a frank dismissal. "No man wants just a bag of bones in bed with
him."

Della was too dumbfound to respond, but Maude
went on as if she was used to people holding their
tongue in her presence. "You can make use of anything that's in Vinnie's room. She didn't have much.
Sent most of her earnings back to Chicago." Maude
pursed her broad red lips. "Told her she was a fool.
You got family, Della?"

"No." *What would her sensible Aunt Frances have
made of all of this?*

"Nobody?" the madam demanded in a doubtful
tone. "Your parents?"

Della swallowed back *They were killed in an auto-
mobile accident.* "They've passed away."

"Anybody else? Brothers . . . sisters?"

"My sister died a couple of years ago. And the aunt
who raised me passed away last summer." She moistened her lips. "I'm alone."

Maude nodded, looking satisfied. Obviously she
liked her employees unattached, thought Della. She
had goose bumps just thinking about working for this
woman. No, she couldn't do it. The whole idea of
keeping track of johns and tricks turned her stomach.

Colin sent her another warning look. *Stay calm.
Don't panic.*

She drew in a deep breath and squared her shoulders. All right, she'd keep her promise to play along.
Taking orders from this hard-nosed businesswoman
would not be easy. She'd have to watch herself. How

long would she be able to pretend to be something that she wasn't? A subservient attitude was not part of her makeup.

Maude spent five minutes warning her about checking invoices and bills. "Damn grocers will cheat you at every turn. Charge you double if they get the chance. Check everything. You foul up...and it comes out of your wages."

Della bit back a sharp retort and glanced at Colin. He was standing rigidly in front of Maude's desk staring down at a newspaper. He pointed to a head-line. "City Councilman Delaney Buying Market Street Property," he read aloud.

"Your—" His pointed glare stopped her from say-ing "great-grandfather."

Maude took the newspaper out of his hand. She snorted when she saw what he had been reading. "Shawn Delaney. Damn politician. Trying to get his hands on every business on the Row. Made a ridicu-lous offer for my place. I dealt with the likes of him in Chicago. Mob bosses, we called 'em, trying to move in."

Colin's expression was as dark as a mine pit. "Is that what he's trying to do...move in?"

"Hell, yes," she swore. "But he'll find out soon enough that we know how to deal with his kind. More than one of them politicians have learned the hard way not to mess with people's livelihoods."

Colin's great-grandfather had been killed on Mar-ket Street...on the doorstep of this very house. There had been no record of who had buried a knife in Shawn Delaney's back. Della's stomach tightened with apprehension. If the freak time warp continued, Colin might be on the spot to find out exactly who had murdered his great-grandfather. Did his dark brooding expression mean that he was thinking the same thing?

Maude eased her bulk into a huge chair behind her desk. "Now listen up, Colin. Tomorrow night, I want you walking around and keeping your eyes open. I want you to stop any fracas before it gets started. The girls get a cut on the drinks, so we don't mind customers getting drunk as long as they don't try to tear up the place. It'll be your job to get a boozer out the front door before he causes any trouble." She gave Colin's strong Celtic features and muscular frame the once-over. She pursed her thick lips. "I don't put up with anyone hassling my girls. And that means you, too. Got it?"

He nodded.

"Report to me in the morning. There's produce to be picked up and furniture to be moved for the night's entertainment." She went on listing all the jobs she expected him to do that ran the gamut from daytime handyman and deliveryman, to nighttime bouncer and bartender.

"For a dollar a day?" He asked in disbelief.

"You want the job or not?"

Della watched the cords in Colin's neck tighten. Being subservient was not in his nature, either. How long would he last under Maude's callused thumb?

"I'll take the job... for now."

"Good." Maude's smile showed her satisfaction. "Gertrude Katz runs the boardinghouse next door. Tell Trudie to give you a room. Most people on Market Street do my bidding…police included. They don't call me Queenie for nothing."

"I can see that," said Colin with an edge of sarcasm to his tone.

Maude didn't seem to notice. "As for you, Della, you'd better get yourself some sleep and act lively tomorrow. The girls haven't been paid for nearly a week. Usually, each night's receipts is figured and pay envelopes slipped under their doors the next morning. Got it? I expect you to get the books in shape in quick order. I've got bills to settle. We'll go over everything in the morning."

Della clasped her hands so tightly that her nails bit into her flesh. She welcomed the pain. It was real. More real than anything in the room.

Maude lifted her ponderous body to her feet. "Have to keep a check on my guests. I keep a short rein on my boarders…and my help." She added the last with a pointed look at Colin. "Remember, no men beyond this room. If you're thinking about putting your shoes under her bed, you've got the wrong floor. I never allow pleasure to be mixed with business. Better hie yourself over to Trudie's and get a room."

"I will…in a minute," Colin answered firmly. "I have a few things I want to say to Della."

Something in his tone made Maude's hard eyes swing from him to Della and back again. The bridge of her nose narrowed and her ugly nostrils flared. "Keep the rules or out you both go. Nobody plays free and easy with me. You try and fox me and you'll be like a dog with his tail cut off behind his ears. Five minutes and then you git!"

With a swish of her taffeta skirt and hidden petticoats, the madam rolled out of the room like a frigate and disappeared down the hall. They could hear her raised voice ordering more food trays from the kitchen.

Colin turned to Della. "Are you all right?"

Her answer was a shudder that racked her slender body. He reached out and drew her against his solid chest. With a sob, she melted against him. He could feel her pulse beating wildly, and through the layers of clothing, the supple curves and lines of her body brought a fierce heat radiating through him. "It's going to be all right, I promise," he said in a husky voice.

"How could this have happened?" Hot tears spilled from her eyes. "What are we going to do?"

He touched her wet cheek. His embrace tightened. He had to get her out of this. He stroked her soft hair and allowed himself a fleeting fantasy of claiming every inch of her utterly feminine body. Then he gave himself a curt rebuke. Della Arnell wasn't for the likes of him. Look what had happened because he had brought her into his life. It didn't matter what happened to him, but he had to protect her at all costs. "The way things are set up we've got a good cover for as long as we want."

"As long as we want," she repeated. She lifted her face and stared at him. Fear, disbelief and anger formed a hard lump in her throat. "We have to find a way back *now*."

"That may not be possible . . . for a little while."

A moment ago she had felt safe in his arms, now she felt trapped. She drew away, glaring at him with frightened eyes. Her voice trembled. "Why did you rush into that tunnel like a crazed man?"

His dark eyes burned into hers. "I didn't have a choice then, and I don't have one now. But I didn't mean for this to happen. Hell, I would send you back in a minute if I knew how."

"What about you?" Her voice rose. "You're not going back, are you?" She recoiled from the steel hardness that turned the blue of his eyes into obsidian. "You wouldn't leave if you could," she said in horror.

"You have to understand. I can't leave until I find some answers."

"Answers to what?"

"The kind of experiences you've been having are not new to me," he said patiently. "All my life, I've had these . . . spells. My mother said I was possessed, that the devil was trying to claim me through the spirit of my great-grandfather. I know it doesn't make sense, but for some reason I've been drawn back into his lifetime. I've never hated anyone as much as I've hated Shawn Delaney and the heredity he gave me."

"Well, I'm not staying. Do you hear me? I'm not going to wait for you to dig up your family's skeletons. I'll find the tunnel. Somebody will believe me . . ."

He grabbed her as she tried to jerk away. This time, his hands on her shoulders were not soft and reassuring but bit harshly into her flesh. "You can't start blabbing about a tunnel. You can't draw attention to yourself. They'll never believe the truth and there's no telling what Maude would do."

"I can't stay here. I can't!"

"I promise you, I'll look around tonight...then we can decide what to do. Trust me," he said again.

"Trust you? How can I? I saw the way you looked at that newspaper. You have some crazy idea of solving your great-grandfather's murder. That's what this is all about, isn't it?"

"I don't know what you mean."

"Don't bother to deny it." She met his gaze squarely as she moved out of his arms. "I recognize a man with a purpose when I see one."

The cleft in his chin deepened. "I have to know what kind of man Shawn Delaney was...why he was murdered. If I understand, perhaps I can lay some demons to rest—"

"Or be killed yourself," she interrupted.

He gave a dismissive wave of his hand. "Not possible. I didn't live in my great-grandfather's day."

With a tremor in her voice, she corrected him. "You do now."

Chapter 4

When Della awoke the next morning, she kept her eyes closed, praying that when she opened them, she would find herself back in her hotel apartment. Her heartbeat quickened as she slowly lifted her eyelids. Disappointment laced with anxiety instantly surged through her. Nothing had changed since last night. She was still wearing a cotton shift for a nightgown, still sleeping in a room that had belonged to the deceased bookkeeper, Vinetta Gray, and still caught in the weird time warp that had swept her back to the turn of the century.

Last night, Colin had promised to come for her if he was successful in his search for the tunnel. She had lain awake for hours, waiting, but he hadn't come. Had he failed to find the tunnel? Or had he lied to her about looking for it? Her feelings for him were in a hopeless tangle. When he held her close, she wanted to lose herself in his embrace. Her pulse leapt when his resonant voice softened to liquid. His intensity, dark passion and compelling personality were mesmerizing. She wondered if she'd be able to leave him behind as she had threatened.

Sitting up in bed, she looked around the room. Everything was just as Vinetta had left it, she recalled with a slight prickling chill. An ugly bowed dresser stood against one wall next to a scarred clothespress whose warped door was slightly open, revealing a collection of clothes. Positioned on one side of a small fireplace was an overstuffed chair with ecru doilies over the headrest and arms. A worn floral rug lay on a wide-planked wooden floor, and faded wallpaper in a pink cabbage-rose pattern covered the walls.

Della had a queasy feeling as she took in the dead woman's personal items. A brush and comb with strands of brown hair still clinging to it lay beside a hand mirror and a box of large hairpins. A porcelain tea set, a leather-bound book and a pair of reading glasses lay on a round drop-leaf table covered with an embroidered fringed cloth. Vinetta Gray was dead but everything was neat and orderly, as if she would return any moment.

Abruptly, Della felt a swish of cold air upon her cheek. *You don't belong here,* a voice whispered. She raised her hands to protect herself from the angry words and cried out as a vile wind of hostility whipped around the room, tossing the lacy curtains with wild frenzy. The sweet smell of lilac perfume was suddenly suffocating and overwhelming. *Go back where you belong!*

Gasping for air, Della leapt from the bed, ran to the door and jerked it open. She leaned weakly against the wall in the hallway, waiting for her legs to regain some strength and her head to quit spinning.

"You ain't coming to breakfast in your shift, are you?" A large Swedish-looking woman with thick blond braids wrapped around her head stood in the kitchen doorway, wiping her hands on her apron. "Miss Vinetta never poked her nose out the door without every hair in place and her dress crinkling with fresh starch."

Della tried to find her voice but couldn't.

The woman gave a disgusted snort. "So you're the new bookkeeper. You looked mighty peaked to me. Too much to drink, I'll wager." The cook's expression showed her disapproval. "If you're looking for the bathroom, it's last door on the right. I guess Miss Maude told you that you're sharing the bathroom. I'm Inga and Lolly's the housemaid. We don't run around half-dressed the way the girls do upstairs. You'd better find a wrapper to cover yerself."

But I don't have any clothes. Della bit back the excuse. The cook's scowl told her she was in enemy territory. *Be careful. Don't give yourself away.* Any kind of scene would arouse suspicions. A hundred questions stabbed at her, but Inga had a closed expression which discouraged any explanations or confidences about insidious perfume and threatening spirits.

"I don't hold breakfast. If it's cold, it's cold," Inga snapped at Della. "Better get a move on. Maude doesn't like to be kept waiting."

Della's breath slowly came back and the suffocating feeling faded. She looked down at the thin cotton

shift that barely covered her. When she had undressed the night before, she'd draped the unfamiliar
clothes over a chair. She couldn't go anywhere the way
she was.

"Well, what you waiting for?" the cook demanded
ungraciously.

Della straightened and glanced through the open
door into the loathsome bedroom. She had no choice
but to go in and get some clothes on. Cautiously, she
took a step inside the door, stopped and waited. She
braced herself for the malevolent whirlwind that had
sent her rushing out into the hall. Nothing. No scent
of lilacs. No vindictive accusations. No hint of hostility. Nothing to indicate that the horrible experience
had been anything but her imagination. She brushed
her hand across her forehead and found it moist with
sweat.

She walked across the room and with trembling
hands, gathered up the dark brown dress, full petti-
coat, knee-length drawers and thick white stockings.
She looked warily at the ribbed corset and left it lying
on the chair. There was no way she was going to wear
such a torturous atrocity. The dress with its long
sleeves and high neck was uncomfortable enough.

With her arms filled with the clothes and the pair of
old-fashioned shoes she'd worn yesterday, she opened
the bedroom door again and peered out. No sign of
Inga. She could hear pans and dishes rattling. A low
murmur of voices floated through the kitchen doorway. She hurried down the hall in bare feet and cotton shift.

Much to Della's surprise, the bathroom was as large
as Vinetta's room. A beautiful marble cabinet con-

tained a small sink and a huge claw-footed tub was raised on a small platform. A smile crossed her lips as she viewed the toilet with its wooden box overhead, a long chain dangling beside it.

Someone had set out sweet-smelling towels and she decided that a quick bath in the deep tub might restore her frayed nerves. She filled it with enough water to touch her chin. The water was only tepid, but running water of any temperature must be a luxury, she mused as she scrubbed with a bar of coal tar soap. Thank heavens, electricity had come into use by the 1880s. The thought startled her. Was she beginning to accept the impossible? Was she really going to be living a hundred years in the past? She reached for one of the large towels and shivered as she stepped out of the tub.

She hated putting on the same undergarments and dress but she had no choice. Using a large-toothed ivory comb lying on the marble counter, she smoothed her fair hair into a French roll and fastened it with several large hairpins from a glass jar that stood beside a bottle of lime juice and glycerin lotion.

A round mirror above the sink had lost some of its silver and gave back a distorted reflection, which made her feel more off-balance than ever. A sob caught in her throat. How could she hold on to her real identity when everything and everyone around her denied it? Where was Colin? She needed his enveloping presence to keep herself sane.

She left the bathroom, walked down the hall past her room and felt a quiver of uneasiness as she entered a large kitchen. Her breath caught when she saw the mess left by last night's activities. Dirty glasses, soiled plates, trays of party food, spotted table linens and crusted silverware covered work counters and one long table that stretched the length of the room.

A dark-skinned girl about sixteen years of age was bending over a big sink. Her chubby arms were buried up to her elbows in soapy water as she washed dirty pots and pans. She didn't look up or give any indication she was aware of Della's presence.

Inga, the cook, came out of the pantry, dangling a duck carcass in each hand. Without acknowledging Della's presence, she plopped down on a stool, dunked one of the fowl into a pan of hot water and started plucking. The smell of wet feathers filled the kitchen.

Della was about to cover her nose with her hand, when Inga stopped a moment and nodded toward a tray sitting at the end of the long table. "Miss Vinetta always took her breakfast at her desk."

I can see why, thought Della, her empty stomach churning from the obnoxious kitchen smells.

"The tea's probably cold by now," the cook said with an edge of satisfaction in her voice.

Della swallowed back a request for a hot cup of coffee. She'd never liked tea, iced or otherwise, but she reminded herself that cold tea was a small price to pay to avoid a confrontation with the formidable cook.

Ignoring the woman's pointed scrutiny, Della picked up the tray and left the kitchen. She walked down a center hall, peering into dark, shuttered rooms as she passed. The somber silent atmosphere in the house was oppressive, a sharp contrast to the bawdy noise and laughter that had filled it the evening before.

When she came to Maude's shadowy office, she put the breakfast tray down on the small desk the madam had pointed out to her. A musty smell permeated the room. Della knew that she would have a headache in short order if she spent any time in the gloomy office. The room was like a closed box with no movement of air.

Going over to a pair of tall windows, she pulled back heavy green draperies, which allowed muted sunlight through floor-length ecru lace curtains. She broke two fingernails trying in vain to open a window to get some fresh air. The thick wooden frames looked as if they had remained shut since the house was built.

She looked out the window at a two-story clapboard house on the other side of a small alley running between the two houses. Gertrude Katz's boardinghouse? Is that where Colin had spent the night?

A spurt of anxiety made Della bite her lip. He had told her to stay put until he found out what was going on, but what if he had disappeared and left her here? She'd always prided herself on her ability to solve her own problems, in any situation, but this was beyond anything she could have imagined.

Turning away from the window, she fought back an impulse to go running out of the house in an effort to find him. He was her anchor, her only hold on reality. She needed to tell him about the hostile presence in Vinetta's room. Last night, he had handled an impossible situation with a deftness that was almost frightening. She had felt an intense pulsating energy radiating from him that both attracted and repelled her. Remembering how his dark looks had been enhanced by the old-fashioned clothes, a new sense of uneasiness brought a dryness to her throat.

She sat down at the small desk and lifted the damask napkin on the breakfast tray which held a small two-cup teapot, a matching cup and one slice of buttered toast on a plate. Nothing else. Either Miss Vinetta had been laced too tightly to eat anything more for breakfast, or she'd had the appetite of a bird, thought Della, her stomach rumbling with emptiness. She was tempted to take the tray back to the kitchen and demand a decent breakfast, but the impulse was short-lived. She wasn't up to another exchange with Inga.

The day had just begun and already she felt bone weary. She sipped the lukewarm tea and had just taken the last bite of toast when a big rough-looking man sporting a full black beard strode into the room.

"I'll be damned," he swore with thick moist lips when he saw Della. He wore a gray-striped suit stretched out at the knees and slightly worn at the wrists. "What the hell we got here?" He strode over to the desk and leered down at her.

Della's mouth went dry as he stood over her, his breath smelling of stale beer. She swallowed the last piece of toast, which seemed to grow in size as it went down her throat.

"Bet my britches you're the new bookkeeper. Well, I'll be damned." His dark eyes took on a lustful sheen as he looked her over. "I haven't seen corn-silk hair any prettier than that. A step up from that dried prune, Vinetta, aren't you, sweetheart?"

"And just who are you?" Della asked coolly.

He fingered the gold chain of his pocket watch and stuck out his beer belly. "Maude's ever-lovin', Jack Gilly."

"Her husband?"

"Husband?" He snorted. "Hell, no. If I'd married Maudie, she'd have hog-tied me long ago for sure. As it is, she has to keep me happy to keep me around. Gives me plenty of room to roam, you know." He plopped a fat buttock on the corner of her desk.

His smirking smile was repulsive and his sour beer breath turned her stomach. She wanted to give him a shove that would send him tumbling off his perch. Everything about him was offensive, his looks, his crude manner, his thick wet lips and roving eyes. "I have work to do," she said ungraciously and leveled her drop-dead look on him.

"We all have work to do, sweetheart." He laughed at some private joke. "I guess you might say *my* job is keeping the old gal thinking she's still a spring chicken. Been doing it for years...off and on. Oh, hell, I take off now and again, but always come back to dear old Maudie."

For a second, Della's curiosity won out over her repulsion. "You've known her for a long time?"

"Hell, yes. Ever since she had her place in Chicago...about seventeen years ago, I guess. Maude wasn't bad-looking back then. Hell, I might even have married her, but she up and left her business and moved West. I guess she thought it was all over between us." He gave a satisfied grunt. "A couple of years later, I surprised her and showed up in good old Denver. Been parking my carcass under her roof ever since."

Della was even more repulsed than ever. He had verified her instinctive dislike. The smirking, foul-smelling Jack Gilly had opened his big ugly mouth and told her exactly what he was...a disgusting, sordid leech!

"'Course, I keep the boarders company. You know what I mean?" he bragged as if her silence meant approval. "Part of my duties as man of the house." He reached out and pinched her cheek. "You stick with good old Jack and you can have the run of this place. Know what I mean? How about a little kiss—"

"Keep your hands off her!"

At the sound of Colin's angry voice, Jack swung off the desk. He planted his stocky legs on the floor and balled his fists as Colin strode into the room.

"Leave her alone."

Jack's mouth spread in a smile above his dark beard as if a good fight was the perfect way to start the day. "Sez who?" He bounced on the balls of his feet, clenched fists ready to meet Colin head-on. Colin's face was dark with rage.

"No...don't!" Della cried. "No, Colin, he'll—" She never got the next word out.

Without slowing his stride, Colin plowed right into Jack's prizefighter stance. Apparently surprised by the rush that resembled a charging buffalo, Jack didn't move fast enough. He staggered backward and Colin landed two hard blows to his stomach.

Jack's eyes bulged and he gasped for air. While he was still off-balance, Colin gave him a shove that propelled him over a footstool and landed him flat on his broad back. Then Colin stood over him, his fists clenched, waiting for the burly man to get up.

A husky laugh from the doorway broke the silence. Maude gave Colin a satisfied nod as she marched into the office. "Guess I've hired myself a good bouncer, all right. If you can take down Jack, you can handle a couple of drunkards with one hand."

Della was relieved but still frightened. Things could have turned out differently. Colin might have been knocked out or beaten up. When he turned to her, his eyes burned with a concern and protective determination that sent a wave of emotion surging through her.

"Are you all right?" he asked anxiously. "I've been worried." Dark shadows lay upon his cheeks, making his eyes seem more deep-set than ever, and a tired stiffness edged his mouth and cheeks.

For a long moment, an intimate wordless communication passed between them. Whatever happened, they were in it together.

"Don't worry, I'm fine," she lied. He looked as if he'd been up all night. She wanted to ask him if he'd located the tunnel but she held back. The deep furrows in his forehead were not reassuring.

Maude stood over Jack. "Get up, you skirt chaser. I don't need to ask what this was all about. Can't keep your eyes off any new gal, can ya? Well, Della's not a boarder. She's my new bookkeeper and you'd better keep your tomcatting away from her. Don't know why I don't kick your backside out the door and be done with it."

Jack got clumsily to his feet and pulled down his vest, which had ridden up over his beer belly. He smoothed his black hair and beard and gave her one of his moist smiles. "Ah, Maudie, you got this all wrong. I was just saying hello to the lady. Nothing to get all steamed up about." He glared at Colin. "Who in the hell is he?" Jack's cold eyes promised that he'd settle with Colin later.

"My new bouncer, Colin. Now get your face out of my office, Jack. Take Billy and the buckboard and pick up the day's deliveries. Inga needs to get started on tonight's menu."

"Don't be giving me orders like I'm a delivery boy," he growled. "You better watch it, Maudie, or I'll head back to Chicago. You'll end up sick again and I won't be around this time to hold things together for you."

"Good riddance, I'd say." But his threat had faded the color in her broad sagging face. Even with rouged cheeks and heavy pink powder, her complexion blanched to an unhealthy pallor. His threat to leave her had met its mark. The woman's icy gray eyes held a hint of fear as Jack stomped out of the room.

Colin raised an eyebrow and exchanged glances with Della. *Maude Mullen had an Achilles' heel.* For whatever reason, she was afraid of losing Jack Gilly.

The woman must be in love with the creep, thought Della. He'd made no bones about following her here from Chicago. How could she be so hard and self-serving about everything else and let a bum like Jack Gilly live off of her?

"Enough of this dillydallying," Maude snapped. "There's work to be done. Colin, move a piano into the red drawing room and set up about thirty chairs in a double circle. We're having live music tonight. Should pack the house. Word's getting out that the Pleasure House knows how to entertain. Open the doors into the next room and clear the floor for dancing, got it?"

When Colin didn't move immediately, she swore. "Dammit, get to work. What are you waiting for?" She glanced at Della. "I warned the both of you. Now git!"

"I need to talk to Della a minute," Colin said firmly. Ignoring Maude's acid stare, he moved to Della's side and asked quietly, "Are you settled in all right?"

No, I'm not settled in at all, she silently answered. She wanted to tell him about the bizarre feeling she'd had that morning. Maybe he could explain the hostility she'd felt in the room and the overpowering scent of lilac perfume. He was the only one who could give her some reassurance that she wasn't losing her mind. She opened her mouth and then closed it. She couldn't say anything with Maude only a few feet away. "I'm doing...okay." She suddenly realized that he had changed clothes. He wasn't wearing the same outfit he'd had on last night. Her gaze went over the blue cotton work shirt and serviceable dark pants. "Where did you get those?"

"Trudie, the landlady of the boardinghouse next door, gave them to me. It's surprising how well they fit."

"Yes, isn't it?" she said as a wintry chill suddenly prickled her skin. Once again she felt that he was in harmony with their surroundings. She gave a quick glance at Maude and then whispered, "Did you look for the—"

"Yes. No luck."

"But—"

"I know." His eyes narrowed. "Try to relax."

Her lips quivered and he touched them gently with his forefinger. "Just hang in there...and don't leave the house."

Maude's long nose quivered with impatience. "Let's get something straight. If you two are working for me, you'll darn well earn your keep. No sparkin' between the two of you except on your free time. That'll be Sunday. Got that? Otherwise, the two of you can leave right now. I'm running a business here. If you've changed your mind about staying, leave. The sooner the better."

· Colin answered evenly, "We'll be staying." He gave Della's arm a meaningful touch. "We'll talk later."

"Much later," Maude growled as he left the room. She began moving things around on her desk. "Let's get at it. We've wasted enough time." She sat down heavily in her chair.

Della tried to put her whirling thoughts in some order. Was Colin telling her the truth? Had he really failed to find the tunnel? Was he lying to her?

"Come here. I'll show you what has to be done."

"Yes, ma'am," Della murmured with what she hoped was a proper degree of subservience. She had no choice but to play the part. For the moment, she was employed as a bookkeeper in a house of ill repute and in spite of herself, she was a little curious to know what the challenges would be.

Maude's ruddy face hardened. "Damn nuisance, Vinetta's passing over so suddenly. Not more than forty, she was. Worked for me for some twenty years."

"That's a long time," Della said, her stomach feeling squeamish, remembering the hostile communication that morning. *You don't belong here.*

"Blasted woman. You'd have thought Maude's Pleasure House was her baby. Damned possessive, she was. Had a temper as quick as gunpowder. She served time when she was only eighteen or nineteen for killing someone in a fit of temper. They let her off with a light sentence because she claimed self-defense. More than once I thought she was going to run a hat pin through any gal she caught snooping around her desk. Hated anyone touching those ledgers of hers."

Della put a hand against the desk to steady herself.

"Now what in the hell's the matter with you?" Maude demanded. "You look sickly."

Della's stomach churned. The smell of lilac perfume was overpowering.

Chapter 5

"What's the matter with you?" Maude demanded again.

"It's that...perfume," stammered Della. "Li-lac."

Maude shrugged. "Vinnie must have left one of her hankies in her desk. She used to reek to high heaven of that sweet scent. You could always tell when Vinetta was around. I guess I got used to it. I don't smell a thing." She gave a dismissive wave of her hand.

The odor was too strong for its source to be a perfumed handkerchief, thought Della. *You could always tell when Vinetta was around.* Maude's words brought new meaning to the bizarre lilac smell. A cold shiver trickled along Della's spine. The woman's spirit must be lingering in the house, thought Della. *A vindictive ghost who knows I don't belong here.* Everyone else might accept her role as Maude's new bookkeeper, but not Vinetta. Della was sickened by the hostility that filled the room, as strong as the sweet scent assaulting her nose.

"Tell me about Vinetta. What was she like?" Della asked, desperate to know more about the woman whose job she was taking and whose vengeful spirit had made itself known to her.

"What do you mean, what was she like?" Maude responded impatiently.

"Did she like . . . people?"

"Vinnie kept to herself and expected everyone else to do the same. And she was a hell of a lot smarter than most people gave her credit for. We got along fine. She knew what her job was and she did it," Maude said pointedly.

"Was she a vindictive person?" Della shuddered, experiencing the cold hostility.

"If you mean, did she always get even, you'd better believe it. Nobody crossed Vinnie. I felt sorry for some of the gals who got sidewise with her." Maude glared at Della. "But she was a damn good bookkeeper. I hired her right out of prison, only twenty years old, she was. Hard and bent like a horseshoe. Had a good head for figures, though. Spent her time in the jug learning bookkeeping. She balanced out every month to the penny. And you'd better do the same," she warned. Maude shifted her plump buttocks and unlocked a desk drawer. She took out a money bag and dumped coins and green currency in a pile. "Pay attention. I don't intend to go over this stuff more than once."

The next two hours were the most intense Della had ever spent. She forced herself to concentrate. The perfume scent faded and with it all hints of Vinnie's hostile spirit. Records had to be kept on everything. The charge for a "quick date" with a girl was five dollars, the cost for spending the night was fifteen to thirty dollars. Maude got half of the set fees. Girls were allowed to keep tips or to sell photos of themselves and got a cut on the drinks and splits of champagne they persuaded their guests to buy. The house's take on every girl's earnings was considerable.

"My expenses would choke an elephant," Maude told Della as if reading her thoughts. She showed Della an enormous grocery order for three weeks: steaks, chickens, rump roasts, ducks, rabbits, eggs, cheeses, fresh fruits and vegetables, milk and cream. "I don't stint on meals," she bragged. "My boarders and guests eat well."

"The girls pay rent?" Della asked in surprise as she viewed accounts receivable.

"Of course they pay rent. I told you last night, I'm not running a charity home. I have to hire servants, pay the police, and grease a lot of hands to keep my liquor license, besides footing all the upkeep expenses. And all the extras! Heaven help me. I have to spend money on bail to get the girls out when the police do raid the place. Sometimes I think I'm supporting the whole damn city of Denver."

Della swallowed hard. "Do they do that often...raid the place?"

"Getting worse all the time. A lot of stuff in the newspapers about cleaning up Market Street. Some blasted civic league is headed by a councilman's wife, Edith Delaney. The women have been marching all over the place, waving flags and making goddamn fools of themselves.''

''Shawn Delaney's wife?''

''That's the one. Her husband's a bigwig on the city council. Rumor has it, he's going to run for governor.'' She made an ugly sound with her mouth. ''Trying to get his hands on property in this end of town. He'd better think twice about taking on Market Street if he plans on living long enough to take office.''

The prophecy brought a chill up Della's back. Had this hard-nosed businesswoman stopped Shawn Delaney with a knife to his back? No doubt Maude would do whatever it took to stop anyone threatening to take away her livelihood.

''Why would people vote for him? I mean, wouldn't his interest in this part of town cost him the election?''

Maude's mouth hardened. ''Oh, he's a smart one, all right. Claims he's buying up the saloons and cathouses so he can clean up the place.'' Her gray eyes were pinpoints of honed steel. ''Cleaning up is what he's aiming to do, all right, but not in the way he's telling everybody.''

Della wanted to find out more about Colin's great-grandparents but Maude cut her off before she had a chance to ask any more questions. ''The gals have been waiting for their wages. Put the exact amount of earnings for each boarder in separate envelopes. And don't think you can slip anything by them,'' she warned. ''They keep track in their heads. If you don't want your hair pulled out by the roots, you better be right on the mark with what's owed them. She shoved the money piles at Della. ''Don't even think of skimming off even a penny if you want to keep that scalp of blond hair on your head.''

Della's hands trembled as she sorted the week's take according to what each girl had earned and put the money in a small brown envelope with the girl's name on it. There were fourteen boarders. It wasn't easy to figure out exactly what each girl had earned on the different kinds of dates and drinks. ''I hope that's right,'' Della said apprehensively when she had finished.

''You'd better be right down to the exact penny. Any overpayment comes out of your pocket. Now, take the wage envelopes upstairs and slip them under the proper doors,'' Maude ordered. ''Each of the girls has a trunk where she keeps a lockbox and some of her wardrobe. A trunk is the only thing she brings to the house, and the only thing she takes with her when she leaves.'' Maude eyed Della. ''Where's yours?''

''It's . . . it's coming,'' she lied lamely.

Maude nodded, apparently satisfied. ''Like I told you yesterday, I was going to clean out Vinnie's room but haven't gotten around to it. Make use of any of her stuff.''

Della blanched. She was convinced that the dead woman's spirit had made itself known. No telling what would happen if she dared to make use of any of Vinetta's personal belongings. Could a ghost expose her for the fraud she was?

Maude must have sensed Della's reluctance to use a dead woman's things. She said sharply, ''I don't expect you to have a wardrobe like the girls' but you can't go around looking like a dreary sparrow.'' The twitch of her broad nose told Della what she thought

about the brown dress with its prim white collar.
"Here." She scribbled a name and address on a piece
of paper and handed it to Della. "My dressmaker. I've
made an appointment for you to go see her this afternoon at one o'clock." Then she waved her hand in
dismissal. "Now, deliver those envelopes before the
gals start howling."

The errand seemed simple enough but Della was
worried. She felt a rise of new apprehension. How in
the world would she relate to the young women whose
"quick dates" took them up and down the stairs as
they bedded any paying customer? Would she be able
to keep her mouth shut and hide her indignation at
their life-style? What if she had made a mistake with
someone's wages? She could imagine some hair-
pulling, cat-scratching boarder coming at her with
nails and teeth bared.

With her heart beating like a runaway jackham-
mer, Della left the office and slowly climbed the wide
center stairs. All she knew about illicit houses came
from books or movies. The flutter of apprehension she
felt was laced with curiosity about the forbidden
regions above.

There were eight bedrooms on both the second and
third floors, she discovered. Impressive double doors
closed off one wing, which Della guessed to be
Maude's private quarters. The upper halls were laid
with dark floral carpets and the walls were covered
with red and gold embossed wallpaper. Huge paintings of voluptuous nudes hung from gold-tasseled
cords at the end of each corridor. All of the paintings
of naked women lying on draped couches looked real

in the dim light of the hall and gave Della an eerie feeling as she passed them.

Doors along the narrow passages were closed as she went up and down the halls, carefully checking the list of boarders and room numbers and slipping the corresponding envelope under each door. An unnerving stillness made the house seem like a slumbering beast waiting for the sun to go down before stirring.

Della had delivered all the envelopes when she was surprised to see an open door at the far end of the third-floor hall. Soft singing drew her to the open doorway. When she cautiously peeked in, she saw a young woman sitting in a rocking chair, humming as she stitched a baby's garment.

For a moment, Della didn't know what to do. The sight was so unexpected that Della just stood there, staring. Whatever she had expected to see, this pleasing, tranquil sight wasn't it. The pretty woman wore a voluminous dark blue wrap and was obviously near the end of her pregnancy. Her blond hair was combed loosely down her back and her profile was as delicate as any carved on a cameo.

Della decided to quietly retreat, but before she could move, the woman raised her blue eyes. They widened and a flicker of surprise crossed her pretty face as she saw Della standing there.

"I . . . I'm sorry," Della stammered.

"Oh, hello. Come in, won't you?" There was a tone of wistful hope in the invitation.

Della knew she should make a quick retreat but something made her hesitate. This attractive young woman was the only sign of life in the upper regions of the house. No wonder she was eager for company, thought Della. "Maybe just a minute," she heard herself saying. "I was delivering the wage envelopes."

"Oh, you must be taking Miss Vinetta's place."

"Yes. I'm Della."

"I'm happy to meet you, Della." She held out a slender hand, which felt small and fragile in Della's. "I'm Lilyanne." She nodded to a settee placed near her rocking chair. "Please sit down."

"I can't stay long," Della said as she eased down on the small sofa. Dainty hemstitched pillows and doilies decorated the back and arms and a lovely white crocheted coverlet was folded neatly at one end. The settee would have been an antique lover's dream, Della thought, with a slight touch of envy.

She was surprised to see how nicely the large room was furnished: a brass bed, walnut dresser and a small writing desk. In addition to the rocker and settee, an upholstered armchair stood on each side of the fireplace. A floral rug, lace curtains, wine-colored drapes and two Tiffany lamps made the room a pleasant one. Della wondered how many gentlemen had been entertained in these congenial surroundings.

Lilyanne carefully laid down her sewing on a small marble-topped table. Della searched for something to say. A pregnant woman in a whorehouse spoke for itself. She judged the young woman to be in her early twenties. Della was suddenly reminded of her sister, Brenda, and the trap she'd fallen into when she ran away from home. A bitterness Della hadn't felt for a long time came back to her as she sat across from the pregnant young woman and thought about her younger sister's early death.

"I was just thinking about a cup of tea," Lilyanne said brightly as she moved heavily out of the chair.

"I really shouldn't—"

"Oh, please. It's all brewed and Lolly brought me some extra sticky buns this morning." She flashed Della a smile. "She must have known I was going to have company." Lilyanne moved with a heavy step across to the small fireplace where a kettle sat on an iron trivet over a low-burning flame.

"Let me help." Della got to her feet.

"If you don't mind..."

"Not at all," Della assured her, grateful to have something to do. Having tea and pastry in an 1880s prostitute's room was too bizarre. Too unreal. She couldn't believe it was happening. "Where are the cups?"

"Right over there. On the tea cart." Lilyanne waved a slender hand toward a set of lovely porcelain cups, saucers and matching floral dessert plates.

As they drank and ate, Lilyanne began to chat about the layette she was making. She eagerly showed Della every little embroidered nightgown and baby blanket. The handiwork was exquisite. A lost art, thought Della as she fingered the delicate lacy tatting. "Lovely."

Lilyanne patted her protruding stomach. "Only a month to go. I hope it's a girl." Lilyanne's eyes took on a dreamy look. "He used to tell me that he'd love to have a little girl that looked just like me."

"The father?" Della asked as evenly as she could. She struggled to mask her astonishment.

Lilyanne looked surprised. "Of course the father."

Della regretted her question. Apparently, Lilyanne had been some man's favorite to the exclusion of all others. She wondered how much money Maude had made off the relationship. The madam had told her that men paid extra to have exclusive rights to a special boarder.

"Wouldn't a boy have an easier time of it?" Della asked bluntly. "I mean, it can't be easy raising any child... under these circumstances."

Lilyanne's face clouded. "Maude says I can't keep the baby. She's willing to let me stay here now, but I'll have to pay her back... later."

Della bit down on her teeth to keep back a tirade that very likely would have astounded and befuddled Lilyanne. Exploitation of any kind enraged Della, and the present situation was even more infuriating because there was nothing she could do to change anything. What was going to happen was going to happen, she knew. But although Lilyanne's fate had already been set in time, Della couldn't let it go. "Don't you have some family?"

Lilyanne's face clouded. "I ran away from home... they'd never take me back."

"Maybe they would," Della said quickly. All the heartache that her sister's life-style had caused was suddenly brought back. She remembered how she'd prayed that Brenda would come back home and give her and Aunt Frances a chance to help her in any way they could. But Brenda had stubbornly gone her own way, refusing to change, refusing help, and dying alone in a crack house because of it. "Sometimes families are just waiting for a second chance to... to make things right."

Lilyanne shook her head. "Not my family. I am in disgrace." She touched her swollen stomach.

"But if you told them that you regretted—"

"Regretted? It's too late for regrets. I made my choices." Her pretty chin hardened. "But I'm not going to give up my baby. I'll keep it, somehow."

Della found it difficult to let the subject drop. She wanted to urge the young woman not to let the father off scot-free. Not to let Maude obligate her to a life of prostitution. Look at other options, she wanted to say. Then an inner voice mocked her, *Maybe she doesn't have any other options.* Della held her tongue.

Lilyanne lifted a crocheted cozy off the teapot. "More tea?"

"No, thank you. I guess I'd better get back downstairs." Della regretted having made personal contact with one of Maude's boarders and being drawn into the ugliness of the house.

"Please come back," Lilyanne urged. "I get lonely. The girls are too busy to spend much time with me. And I can't go downstairs the way I am. Maude says it's not good for business."

Della bit back a caustic retort. Maude would undoubtedly carry out her threat to throw Della out in the street if she caused any trouble between the madam and Lilyanne. Besides, there wasn't any way she could fight a system that had been in place over a hundred years ago. Or was there? Could anything be changed? Impulsively, she took Lilyanne's hand, but when she tried to say something to the sweet pregnant woman, no words would come.

"I like you, Della," Lilyanne said simply.

"And I like you." With a choked feeling in her chest, Della left the room and went downstairs. Instead of returning to Maude's office, she began checking the various rooms. Where was Colin? Maude had told him to set up the red drawing room. Della checked all the first-floor parlors but couldn't find him. He must have gone on the errands Maude had given him, she reasoned.

She wandered over to the front door. He was lucky to have an excuse for getting out of the house. Maybe the answer to returning to the twentieth century lay outside Maude's house. Something about Lilyanne's resigned attitude mocked Della's own temerity to take an active role in solving her own situation. She'd never been one to stand around and wait for a problem to solve itself. Even though she knew that she shouldn't chance getting separated from Colin, she turned the brass knob and walked outside.

The bright sun touched her face with reassuring warmth. She filled her lungs with clean fresh air. She stood on the small porch for a moment before she went down the steps and walked to the front sidewalk.

Market Street was bustling with rattling wagons, neighing horses and fast-rolling buggies. A remembered scene came back to Della with the shock of déjà vu. The same sights, the same cacophony of sounds she'd experienced once before—in front of her hotel.

Her hotel.

She stopped and looked across the busy street. There it was. The Denver Railroad Hotel. A lump caught in her throat. *This is the way her hotel looked when it was built.* Fashioned of light gray stone, the hotel's arched windows rose three stories and decorative pillars stood along the front steps holding up a fringed canopy. Through the years, the stone had darkened, the decorative facade of the hotel had disappeared and a side portico where horse-drawn carriages waited had been torn down.

She felt her heart lurch to a stop. Was it possible that she could walk across the street, enter the front door and wander freely through the halls and rooms she knew so well? Could she see for herself the way the hotel had been before the years had transformed it?

She ignored an inner voice warning that the two worlds, then and now, might not mesh. Drawn to the hotel, Della crossed the street, dodging lumbering dray wagons and horse-drawn carriages. When she reached the other side of the street, she hurried down the sidewalk toward the front of the hotel. Before she reached it, a familiar figure got out of a hack at the hotel's entrance.

She couldn't believe her eyes. Colin! She ran forward and caught his arm.

He turned around. "Pardon?"

Stunned, she couldn't speak. The same height, broad shoulders, the same dark wavy hair, but the man was a stranger. His features were heavier. The shape of his face broader.

She must have paled and looked ready to faint.

"Is there something wrong?" he asked.

With great effort, she managed to stammer, "I...I thought you were someone else."

He smiled one of Colin's rare smiles. "My loss." He swept off his hat. "Shawn Delaney, at your service, miss."

Chapter 6

Could this really be happening? She stared at Colin's great-grandfather. Strong eyebrows lifted over the same dark blue eyes as Colin's and raven hair drifted forward upon his forehead in a wave. The shape of his face was different and his features were not as well balanced as Colin's, but to her the family resemblance could not be denied. She fought an impulse to touch his face to reassure herself that he was indeed a stranger.

She wavered and he reached out, putting his hand on her arm to steady her. His hands were larger than Colin's but his fingers were the same long, dexterous-looking shape. He wore a wide wedding ring, scrolled with an elaborate engraving. She drew away from his steadying touch.

"Is something the matter?" he asked in a familiar voice.

I thought you were your great-grandson. The truth would sound like the blubbering of a crazy woman.

"You appear to be distressed, miss. Can I be of help?" He frowned, obviously puzzled by her intense scrutiny.

She knew she should mumble an apology, turn on her heel and leave immediately. Only she couldn't. She remained rooted to the spot and her voice seemed to come from far away. "You should stay away from Market Street, Mr. Delaney. It's... it's not safe." *Someone is going to kill you.*

He raised one black eyebrow. "I'm acquiring property in this area."

"I know," she said with a rush. "But forcing people to sell and taking over their businesses is dangerous." She knew that she was trying to do the impossible, to change history after it had already been made, but she had to say something to warn him. "Why don't you buy property on some other street. Why does it have to be here?"

He gave her a politician's smile. "Because I think the best way to change lower downtown into a respectable business district is to replace Denver's redlight district with honest businesses."

"Some people think that's just a ruse. That you're really setting yourself up to be king of all these illicit activities," she countered, remembering Maude's remarks about him cleaning up.

He frowned as his gaze traveled over her prim dress, bare head and gloveless hands. "May I ask what you're doing in this neighborhood?"

"I..." Her eyes slid to the hotel's entrance.

"If you're thinking of staying at the Railroad Hotel, I would advise against it. You should stay away," he warned.

Something deep within his eyes prickled the skin on her neck.

She swallowed the dry lump in her throat. "Why do you say that?" *Did he know that the future and the past were caught in that hotel?*

He gave her a superficial smile. "It's popular with traveling men and not a place that would be appropriate for a respectable lady such as yourself."

Your warning is too late... or is it too early? What would happen if she told him that she would spend her inheritance on the same hotel, over a hundred years from now? He would think she was crazy. *Maybe I am.* She felt color draining from her face.

"You don't look well," he said. "I'd be happy to recommend more suitable accommodations, miss—"

"Della Arnell," she managed to say in an unsteady voice.

He held out his hand. "I'm happy to make your acquaintance, Miss Arnell."

Cautiously, she put her hand in his. His clasp was warm and firm. He was no figment of her imagination. His fingers tightened and suddenly he was standing close enough for her to smell the bay rum tonic on his hair. His dark eyes were puzzled as they searched her face. "Have we met before?"

"No. Never." The bewildering overlap of Delaney men generations apart made her jerk her hand away.

"Strange," he mused aloud, frowning slightly.

"I...I have to go."

"Wait a minute, Miss Arnell. I want to—"

She didn't wait to hear the rest as warning signals went off in her head. She had to get away from Shawn Delaney and the hotel. He had warned her that it would be dangerous for her to go inside and she believed him.

Rushing blindly across the street, she nearly collided with a mule pulling a vegetable cart. The husky driver yelled an obscenity at her before she made it safely to the sidewalk in front of Maude's house.

She hurried up the porch steps. When she reached the front door, she turned and looked back across the street. Shawn Delaney was still standing there, watching her. Even in the bright sunlight, she felt a bone-deep chill. From this distance, it could have been Colin studying her. Was Colin Delaney actually a figure from the past? And not from the twentieth century at all? *Was he the one who was going to be murdered on this very doorstep?*

Della shut the front door and leaned against it, her forehead beaded with moisture and her lips trembling.

"Della?"

Colin's voice? Or the man she had just left across the street? Was the sound of her name only in her head? She couldn't be sure.

"Are you all right?" The muted light through the etched-glass doors touched Colin's face as he came toward her. She gave a whimper and went into his arms. "It's you," she whispered with relief.

He gathered her close and touched her moist forehead. "Are you ill?"

Ill? If only the answer were that simple. A couple of pills and some rest and all would be normal again. She fought back a wave of hysterics.

"What is it? What's happened? Where have you been? I told you not to go out of the house."

"I know but I..." she faltered. "Inside... outside...it doesn't matter! I can't make sense of any of this."

He put his arm around her shoulder and led her into the front parlor where he had been moving a piano and chairs as Maude had directed. Easing her onto one of the red plush sofas, he sat down beside her. "Now, tell me. Where have you been? What happened?"

She touched his face with trembling fingers, tracing the hard curves of his cheeks and the sensuous lines of his mouth. "I'm not even sure you're you!"

He took her hand from her face and kissed her fingertips. Then he gently took her face in his hands and gave her one of his rare smiles. Slowly and deliberately, he lowered his mouth to hers, kissing her gently at first, teasing her lips, urging her mouth to open to his. His tongue danced along her lips, deliberately tugging, probing and tasting. When he slowly lifted his mouth from hers, they were both breathing heavily. "Does that convince you?"

A tingling warmth flowed through her body like liquid. Her breath was short. When she didn't answer, he challenged her. "Not convincing enough?"

Before she could catch her shaky breath, he kissed her again. At the same time that his mouth claimed hers, his hands slipped down and found her full ripe breasts. His thumb pressed against the soft cloth of her bodice, lightly teasing the hidden nipple into a hardening peak.

She gasped as spirals of pleasure shot through her. Her arms stole around his neck. She slipped her fingers through the thick strands of his hair and locked her hands at the base of his neck. Closing her eyes, she returned his kisses greedily, blocking out everything in her mind except the heated hunger unleashed between them.

He drew away first. "You should have warned me about the smoldering volcano hidden under that controlled exterior of yours," he said hoarsely.

She laughed softly, surprised. She didn't consider herself to be an erotic female in any sense of the word. But she'd never before experienced such abandoned physical desire.

"I felt a pull the first moment you walked into my office asking about the hotel," Colin confessed. "I tried to lie to myself. Pretend that you could never be an important part of my life. And now..." He kissed her again with a fierceness that startled him. He was a fool. She had no place in his life. He'd never share his heritage of pain and hatred with anyone so honest and brave.

When he lifted his lips, she was filled with a new anxiety that somehow he was caught in a time loop that threatened his life as well as his great-grandfather's. "I met Shawn Delaney just now and—"

"You what?" He felt as if she'd landed a blow to his stomach. "Where?"

"Across the street... in front of the hotel."

"Are you sure it was him?"

"I'm sure." She moistened her lips. "I saw a family resemblance between you. The same color hair and physical build. Penetrating blue eyes. Nobody else might notice it because his face is broader and his features are heavier, but your voices sound very much the same. I . . . I tried to warn him about buying property on this street. I know it was stupid," she admitted, wishing that she'd kept the whole bizarre encounter to herself. Colin had lost all the gentle caring of a lover, and an explosive intensity radiated from him.

"Did he talk to you?" he asked, anxiety in his tone, every muscle in his body rigid.

"He warned me to stay away from the hotel. I think he may have been one of the ghostly figures I saw wandering in the halls."

She moistened her lips. "I had the feeling that he was aware of some strange rapport between us."

"Damn him!" Colin raked his hair with his hand. "I never meant to drag you into my sordid history. I never wanted this to happen."

Della was stunned by the black fury that leapt into his eyes. A moment ago, she and Colin had been locked in a passionate embrace that had shut out everything else. Now they were separated by a destructive chasm she didn't understand. She took his hand and held it tightly. "Tell me. Tell me about your family. About your mother. You can't shut me out. Not now."

A weariness crept into his voice. "If only I could. The first time you came into my office, I thought the nightmare of my life was over. I honestly believed that putting the hotel in your hands would change everything. If only that tunnel hadn't been found, all of this wouldn't have happened."

"There's no way to be sure," she said.

He sighed. "I suppose you're right. When I was growing up, my mother built a terror in me that I could never overcome the evil that had been passed down from my great-grandfather. I've had nightmares, plenty of them. My mother hated my father...my grandfather...and in the end, she hated me, too."

"And she...took her own life?"

He nodded. "She married my father because she was pregnant with me. He was a Delaney and she thought he had money, but my grandfather was still living and my father didn't have anything. My father was not yet twenty-five when he died. My grandfather outlived him by nearly seventy years."

"Did you know your grandfather?"

Colin's mouth tightened in an ugly line. "I met him once. He was an old man then and wouldn't have anything to do with us. Wouldn't give my mother a penny. Ian Delaney was the meanest, tightest, most uncharitable man alive and the slumlord of all Market Street property that he had inherited from his father, Shawn Delaney." Colin gave a hard laugh. "My mother told me all my life that I was a Delaney through and through. She went to her grave predicting I'd turn out no better than they had."

A chill sluiced through Della. She wanted to protest the resignation in his tortured expression. Clearly Colin's mother had used her bitterness as a weapon and had put a load of misplaced guilt upon him. What kind of mother would plant such destructive fears in her own child? Anger made her voice sharp. "I don't believe that genetics dominates our lives. We have the choice and free will to make our lives what we want."

He thought about Elena and the night she had drowned at Echo Lake. They were both seventeen and had been drinking heavily. When someone in the party had suggested a canoe race, he eagerly took the challenge because he was always trying to prove himself. Elena was in the boat with him and they were in the lead when something happened. The boat capsized. Elena had drowned and his youth had been loaded down with guilt. He had sworn never to bring another woman into his life...and then he had met Della. How could he have forgotten that his life was cursed?

"Did you really search for the tunnel last night?" she asked quietly.

"There's no tunnel. At least not that I could find."

"But there has to be. Maybe you didn't look hard enough." She drew back and gave her chin a firm lift. "Whatever strange force brought us here could take us back. There has to be a way to reverse what happened. I'm not giving up. And if I locate the tunnel, I'm going to follow it across the street and..."

"And what?"

Her determination wavered. What if the present and future were really one and the same in some terrifying way? What if she went inside the hotel and became one of the phantom prostitutes, doomed to wander forever in her unfinished hotel? Shawn Delaney had warned her not to go inside. Did he know that disaster would overtake her if she mixed the present and past by going into the hotel? She put her finger against her temples. She couldn't think rationally anymore.

"The safest course is not to force anything," Colin said softly, lowering her hands. "Promise me you'll not do anything rash."

"I can't promise."

Her eyes were clear and truthful. He felt his chest tighten. "What do you mean?"

"If there's a way out, I'm going to take it."

They looked at each other in silence. She searched his face, silently pleading with him to assure her that he would never let her go without him.

Her chest rose with suppressed emotion and he touched her cheek with a caressing finger. He would send her back this minute if he knew the way. "We'll stay together until I can decide what to do," he said, straightening up. "I guess you'd better go with me this afternoon."

"Where?"

"I'm going to pay a visit to my great-grandmother. The Delaney mansion was torn down to make room for a parking lot, but I was there once as a boy. My grandfather, Ian, was an old man and still lived in the house." His voice grew grim. "I remember how terrified I was. And how completely my grandfather humiliated me and my mother."

"Why on earth put yourself through the ordeal of going there again?"

"I have to know what kind of woman married Shawn Delaney."

Della opened her mouth to protest and then closed it again. The determined set of his chin told her it would be a waste of breath. "Did you know that Edith Delaney heads some kind of citizens' organization? At least that's what Maude told me."

He nodded. "That's how I arranged an appointment with her this afternoon...to offer my support to her citizens' league. I suspect the organization is just a front to get political backing for her husband. Anyway, I've ordered a hansom cab for three o'clock. Will you pay a visit to the old Delaney mansion with me?"

She hesitated. "Maude has made an appointment with a dressmaker for this afternoon. An address on Larimer Street."

"What time?"

"One o'clock."

"Why don't I go with you to the dressmaker's and afterward we'll both pay Edith Delaney a visit?"

Della was pulled in two directions. She didn't want to go...but she didn't want him to go without her. "All right."

"Good." He lightly brushed her lips with his and then drew back as if hesitant to ignite the wild hunger that had enveloped them earlier. He walked her down the hall to Maude's office. "See you in a couple of hours."

Della sat down at her desk and put her head in her hands. What possible good could come from Colin's visiting a house that had only held terror for him as a boy? She shivered just thinking about the meeting between him and his great-grandmother, who was almost his same age now, and who had lived over a hundred years earlier.

Chapter 7

Della was seated at her desk working on a pile of receipts that had never been recorded, when a scowling boy, thirteen or fourteen years old, brought in a lunch tray. With a quick belligerent glare in her direction, the youth shoved the tray on her desk and turned to leave without a word. It must have been Vinetta's habit to work through the noon hour, thought Della.

"Wait a minute." She gave the youth a smile which had little effect on his frown. "Thank you. What's your name?"

"Billy."

"Thank you, Billy. I appreciate you bringing in a tray." She silently hoped there was something more substantial than a piece of cold toast under the napkin. "Do you work in the kitchen?"

"I do lots of things," he answered in an antagonistic tone. A ruddy complexion matched thick sandy hair that sprang from his head like uneven straw. His small brown eyes were hard and his glare matched the set of his mouth. "My ma runs this place."

"Oh, you're Maude's son," Della said, hoping her voice didn't reveal her surprise. She never would have guessed that Maude had a kid his age. Maude must have been in her early-thirties when she'd had him, if he was her natural son. "I bet you're a lot of help to her."

He shrugged and stomped out of the room. Was he Jack Gilly's son? The boy didn't resemble him in looks but Billy could have taken after his mother. Maude, Jack and Billy? She couldn't picture the three of them posing for a happy family portrait. She imagined that a rumbling hostility among the three of them would be like a volcano ready to explode. More than ever, she felt that every minute under Maude's roof was filled with danger from every side.

She put aside the ledger and lifted the napkin. Another small pot of tea, a sandwich of cucumber and watercress and one small pickle. Where was all the food listed on the grocery bill? Della ate every crumb and drained the teapot. The meager fare mocked the rumble in her still-empty stomach. Della had never been a big eater but the unsatisfying breakfast and lunch left a gnawing hunger that sent her to the kitchen with a determination to find a decent lunch.

She couldn't believe the change there. Last night's mess had been cleared away and Inga and the dark-skinned girl, Lolly, had been joined by two young girls who looked Asian. The four women moved around the room like a horde of ants, bringing things out from the pantry, slicing vegetables and fruit at worktables

and carrying trays to the dining room. The aroma of
roasting meat and freshly baked bread taunted Della's taste buds as she set down the empty tray in the
midst of the bustle.

Inga had flour up to her elbows as she put finishing
touches on a dozen pies and shouted orders like a
general in charge of troops. ''Put that cream in the
churn . . . get those vegetables boiling . . . don't throw
that stock out! What do you mean you can't find a
colander?'' She slapped a hunk of pastry dough on a
floured board and kneaded it with her large muscular
hands. Then she glared at Della as if she would use the
rolling pin on her if she opened her mouth or came a
step closer to the worktable.

Della's courage deserted her. She was not up to any
kind of confrontation with the bellicose cook. Meekly
she passed through the kitchen and went down the hall
to Vinetta's room.

Opening the door gingerly, she cautiously stepped
inside the room and sniffed. No hint of lilac perfume.
Nothing out of the ordinary. Just a room filled with
the dead woman's possessions. Mentally she chided
herself for giving credence to the presence of Vinetta's ghost, but another part of her accepted the reality
of the lingering malevolent spirit she had felt earlier.

As much as she disliked the idea, Della knew that if
she was going to the Delaney home with Colin, she
needed to look more presentable. That morning, she
had been the only woman on the street not wearing a
hat and gloves, with the chain of a purse hanging on
her arm. Since Maude had told her to help herself to
any of Vinetta's things, she opened the doors of the

old wardrobe and looked through the garments hanging there.

All of the dresses were more attractive than the ugly brown one she wore. A poplin gown made with a spriggy print in shades of blue caught her eye. Della held up the dress and decided, surprisingly, that it looked about the right size. It was fashioned with an overskirt and a saucy bustle in the back. The bodice had a modest neckline and pearl buttons down the front.

A large hatbox on the wardrobe shelf contained two hats, a modest yellow straw that perched on one side of the head and a fancy wide-brimmed hat with a blue bird set in a nest of pink roses. The fancy hat looked brand-new and Della wondered if Vinetta had lacked the courage to wear it. *Had one of the women upstairs given it to her?*

Della put away the elaborate bonnet. The simple straw hat with the small dotted veil would do just fine. She found gloves and a beaded bag in one of the drawers. When she opened the purse, she was surprised to find several silver dollars inside. Her mood brightened. *Food,* she thought. Now she could buy herself a decent meal.

As she changed into the old-fashioned dress, she waited for Vinetta's hostile spirit to show its displeasure, but the room remained free of the odious perfume and any claustrophobic sensation. When she had finished dressing, she looked in the mirror and felt like someone going to a costume party.

When Della met Colin in the entrance hall a few minutes later, his gaze traveled from her blond hair and hat, down over the summer dress that accented her full bust and rounded hips. She peered through the dotted veil and waited anxiously for his reaction. "What do you think?"

"Nice."

"That's it?" She was disappointed. Her feminine vanity wanted him to be more enthusiastic. "Nice?"

"Very nice." There was a soft twinkle in his eyes as he offered his arm with a flourish. "Shall we go walking, my lady?"

Under different circumstances, she would have laughed at their playacting, but once they were out on the street, she found it frightening the way they blended into the long-ago scene. She couldn't believe that nobody stopped to point an accusing finger at them. She was grateful for Colin's steady arm and the easy grace of his stride as he walked beside her.

He had changed into the same dark double-breasted waistcoat, vest and trousers of the night before but had acquired a fresh white shirt and starched collar. He wore a bowler hat on his dark wavy hair that made him look more than ever like Shawn Delaney. Where was he getting his wardrobe?

He read the question in her eyes. "My landlady."

"Trudie Katz?"

He nodded and told her about the spry little German woman who had given him a small room furnished with a nice clean bed, wash table with pitcher and chamber pot.

"Me and Maude have a good arrangement," Gertrude Katz had told him the night before when he had gone across the alley to her boardinghouse. "Maudie throws business my way whenever she can. I was in the trade myself but got too old. Running a boarding-house suits me. Where are your clothes?''

"I'm traveling light," Colin had told her.

She had nodded as if what he said made some kind of sense to her. A few minutes later, she'd returned to his room with two packed valises. "Some freeloader tried to duck out without paying his rent." She gave Colin a toothless grin as she opened the worn leather bags. "Sneaking out a window when I caught him. Looking down the barrel of my shotgun, he decided to leave these behind." As she took out the garments and hung them on a row of nails pounded into the wall, she had nodded knowingly. "A perfect fit if I don't miss my guess."

Even though the sun was warm and bright, Della shivered. The idea that they were wearing clothes that belonged to people who had lived over a hundred years ago made her skin crawl. She drew Colin closer to her side as they walked, and when he looked down at her, his enveloping, caressing eyes brought warmth back into her body.

When they walked past a restaurant called Delmonte of the West, Della stopped abruptly in the middle of the sidewalk. "Let's go in and eat."

"Sorry. I borrowed some change from my landlady to pay for the hansom cab this afternoon...and that's all I have. I've been trying to get my courage up to ask the dragon lady for an advance."

"I've got five dollars," Della told him with a smug grin.

"You didn't steal it from Maude, did you?" he asked anxiously. "She'll call the cops on you without blinking an eye."

"Relax. I didn't steal it." She hesitated. "Well...not exactly."

"What do you mean...not exactly?"

She held up the beaded bag. "I found it in this purse. Maude told me that I could make use of Vinetta's things." Della shrugged. "She probably didn't mean money, but what the heck. I'm starved. All I've had today is lukewarm tea, a piece of cold toast, a cucumber and watercress sandwich and a pickle. I bet you've had more than that."

"I have to admit the meals at the boardinghouse are pretty good. Not fancy food but plenty of it. Trudie brags that her cooking will stick to your ribs."

"No doubt Maude's cook, Inga, is one of the best, but I haven't had a chance to taste any of her culinary achievements. Come on, I'm going to spend Vinetta's hard-earned silver dollars."

Colin glanced at the watch stuck in his vest pocket. "You're going to be late for your appointment."

"I don't care. If I don't get some food, I'll fall on my face before the seamstress has a chance to get out her tape measure."

"All right, lunch, it is." He opened a beveled-glass door etched with silver and gold.

Once inside the elegant restaurant, Della began to have misgivings. Decorative window trimmings, thick floral carpets, delicate frescoes and colorful ceiling murals warned her that she might have been too hasty in insisting upon eating in a fancy establishment like Delmonte's.

"Table for two?" asked a well-groomed maître d' in black attire.

Della sent an anxious glance at Colin. How far would five dollars go in a place like this? He had already warned her that he wouldn't be able to buy lunch.

The maître d' escorted them to a table spread with white linen, bone china plates, silver tableware and etched glassware. Soft piano music played in the background. When a waiter handed Della an engraved menu, she shot an anxious glance down the right side and silently let out her breath. The prices were unbelievably cheap. She sent Colin a relieved smile.

"Five dollars was a lot of money a hundred years ago," he said as if amused by her sudden bright smile.

She took a deep breath and ordered lentil soup, a salad of fresh greens, glazed roast chicken breast, mashed potatoes and gravy and buttered succotash.

"I'll have coffee," Colin told the waiter.

The service was fast and efficient and they didn't do much talking until Della had almost finished her meal.

"How did the morning go with Maude?" Colin asked.

She touched a damask napkin to her lips. "Very enlightening. You wouldn't believe how much money she pays out for protection. I wonder if there's an honest policeman in the whole city." She told him about the financial arrangements that Maude had with her boarders. "She takes half of everything a woman earns. And from what I can tell, the women have to spend most of their earnings on clothes, food and rent."

"Exploitation, pure and simple," Colin agreed.

Della frowned. "I met one of her boarders, Lily-anne, a pregnant woman in her early twenties. Maude's letting Lilyanne live in the house until her baby's born, then she has to work out her indebtedness." Della's eyes flared angrily. "The girl needs a hand up, not someone pushing her farther and farther into the gutter."

"Easy! Don't get involved," he warned. "There's nothing either of us can do about the way Maude exploits people. I'm expected to be a full-time servant during the day and a bouncer till two o'clock in the morning."

"You could quit."

"And go where?" The question created a leaden silence that was broken by a waiter flourishing a large tray of desserts at their table.

Della selected a parfait made with fresh fruit that the waiter said had been brought in by rail from California.

"Feeling better?" Colin asked with an amused glint as she ate the last bite of dessert and sighed contentedly.

"Much."

The bill came to two dollars and seventy-five cents.

They were twenty minutes late for her appointment with Miss Turnball, an emaciated-looking middle-aged woman who lived in two rooms above a pool hall. The seamstress had a tape measure hanging around her neck and several loose strands of thread looped over her head, as if for safekeeping. Her tired expression changed very little when Della made her apologies for being late.

"I think I'll go downstairs to the pool hall while you're busy," Colin said as the two women were about to go into a back room for the fitting.

"I'd rather you didn't," Della said quickly, unreasonable panic rising in her chest.

"Why not?"

She couldn't lose the nagging apprehension that he could disappear at any moment and never come back. "Because... I don't think I'll be that long. Please stay."

"All right, I'll be right here... if you need me." He was surprised at the fear in her eyes. From the first time he'd met Della, she'd flaunted her independence and gone out of her way to show him that she was perfectly capable of taking care of herself. In fact, she had told him that she didn't need a man in her life. But that was before their lives had been turned inside out.

"Thank you." A wave of relief swept her face as he settled himself on an uncomfortable-looking chair and picked up a well-worn issue of the local newspaper.

Della followed the seamstress into a bedroom-sewing room so crowded with material and piles of unfinished garments that a small area in the middle of the floor was the only open space.

Miss Turnball pulled a small stand out from under a loaded table. "Stand on that and I'll get your measurements."

Working like a darting bird, the small woman bobbed around Della, snapping her measuring tape and jotting down numbers on a gray piece of paper. "Maude ordered two dark skirts, white blouses and one tunic jacket."

Della felt a spurt of annoyance. "Does Maude make all the decisions about what her help wears?"

The seamstress nodded. "She chooses the styles, material and number of gowns. She pays for everything and deducts the cost from wages."

"Bondage," Della muttered. Like everyone else in Maude's Pleasure House, she was about to be caught in a debtor's net that would only tighten around her.

"I made the dress you're wearing for Miss Vinetta." Miss Turnball pursed her lips. "It fits you because she laced up tight enough to bring in her waistline two inches. With a proper corset, you could do the same thing and you'd have a dainty waist the envy of everyone in the house." She smiled wanly as if somehow she would be credited with the transformation.

"I would rather be able to breathe and eat," Della said flatly. "The whole idea of rigid corsets is stupid and unhealthy."

Miss Turnball shrugged her tired shoulders as if she'd done her best to correct an improper situation. "I'll have your things ready by the end of next week."

I pray to God I won't be here that long. Was it possible that she and Colin were doomed to live the rest of their lives in a time period that wasn't their own? A sense of urgency hurried her from the room. She saw with relief that Colin was still sitting on the ugly chair.

"Through already?" Colin said with surprise as he tossed down the newspaper and stood up. A comforting warmth sped through her as she slipped her arm through his.

"Thanks for waiting," she said.

"Did you think I wouldn't?" He put his hand over hers.

"I'm not sure about anything or anybody anymore." She gave him a worried smile. *Especially you.*

On their walk back to Market Street, she caught sight of their reflection in store windows. Their slightly distorted and vague images added to the sense of unreality she felt in the unfamiliar surroundings. The hansom cab that Colin had hired to take them to his great-grandfather's home was waiting in front of the boardinghouse when they rounded the corner.

"Good," Colin said.

As he hurried her toward the black, horse-drawn hack, Della held back. "I don't think this is a good idea."

A flicker of impatience crossed his face. "I'll chance it."

She raised her pleading face to his. "Please, Colin. Let it go. Spend your energies on finding a way back to our own time. Let the past stay buried."

"It's never been buried," he countered solemnly. "I've been haunted by my sordid heritage since the day I was born. But it's my family and my quest. There's no need for you to get involved."

She wanted to laugh outright. "Not get involved? Don't you think it's a little late for that?"

"I meant that you can stay on the sidelines," he answered gruffly. "You have every right to turn your back on me and this entire situation."

"Is that what you want?"

"No. But I'll understand." An anguished pain darted in his eyes. "In fact, it might be better if you stayed completely away from me."

"It probably would be," she agreed. "But I don't think that's an option." She sighed. "All right. Let's go."

He helped her into the black leather seat of the cab and then sat beside her. A swarthy driver climbed into a high seat, gave a snap of the long reins and the horse-drawn cab lurched forward. Colin gave Della a reassuring smile, but a tightening in his chest mocked his outward composure.

Della's ears roared with the clanging of electric trolley cars as the hack maneuvered through the congested business district. Vegetable carts of various sizes and shapes lined the sidewalks on both sides. Women customers filled string bags and looked at produce while anxious merchants hovered nearby. Street vendors hawked their wares in loud, raspy voices. A man with a honing wheel was hunkered down on a sidewalk, sharpening knives.

After a few blocks, the clamor of the streets faded and the cab rolled into an elite residential area. Tall trees shaded large, ostentatious mansions built of stone and brick, fashioned with crenellated parapets, Gothic towers, Queen Anne gables and Romanesque arches.

"Beautiful homes, aren't they?" Della said. "There must have been a lot of wealth in Denver when these were built."

"Gold and silver mines poured money into the pockets of men who became millionaires overnight."

"Is that where the Delaney fortune came from?"

He nodded. "Shawn Delaney staked a couple of prospectors who hit it rich. He never had to do anything but rake in the gold." Colin's expression hardened. "My great-grandfather didn't need to corrupt himself or the family by sinking everything into those Market Street properties."

"I don't understand why your grandfather, Ian, held on to them during his day."

"Property values fell. That part of Denver became skid row. The only people who lived there were unfortunates—social outcasts, perverts, alcoholics and the aged who had no other place to go. My grandfather made money from run-down bars, pawnshops and alley hotels. Never put a dime back into the properties. He kicked my father out when he was seventeen and turned away my mother when she came to the house to ask for help."

"How old were you then?"

"About five, I think."

The hack stopped before the driveway of one of the largest mansions on the block. Every muscle tensed in Colin's face as if the forbidding house were emitting some grim communication. Built of gray granite, the mansion stood in the shadows of overhanging tree branches. Neoclassic columns rose three stories to a jagged mansard roof. Chimneys jutted into the air like tentacles and numerous glazed windows stared out like the dull eyes of some mammoth creature. A wrought-iron fence enclosed the grounds and a gate house stood beside a double gate.

A thickset young man with drooping mustache appeared in the gate-house doorway. *Maybe he wouldn't let them in,* Della thought hopefully. She didn't want to go inside the grim, gray house and she feared that Colin would only find more torment in this visit.

The officious-looking guard sauntered over to the cab and peered inside. He scowled as if ready to deal forcibly with their intrusion.

"Mr. Colin and Miss Della Arnell to see Mrs. Delaney," Colin said in an authoritative tone. "We're expected." Colin met the guard's glare straight on.

The man gave an insulting shrug of his shoulders but opened the double iron gates. Della's stomach took a sickening plunge as they clanged shut behind them.

Chapter 8

Colin stared at the large brass lion's head mounted on the front door. He remembered looking up at it when he and his mother had made their only visit to the house. When she had reached for the knocker, he'd been afraid the lion's sharp-toothed mouth would snap shut and bite off her fingers.

Half expecting to be shut up in a cage and fattened up like Hansel and Gretel, he'd been terrified to step inside the house. His mother had repeatedly warned him that his grandfather was a heartless monster who wouldn't hesitate to throw his own flesh and blood to the dogs.

Colin didn't remember much else about the visit except that his mother had shoved him in front of a withered old man who smelled like pond water.

"Look at him," she had shrieked. "Your grandson. He's Delaney through and through, nothing but trouble since the day he was born. Look in his devil's eyes and see for yourself.''

As Colin stood there looking at the ugly brass lion, his mother's shrieking voice came back to him. He felt his insides knot and beads of sweat form on his forehead. She had threatened to kill herself a hundred times, wringing terror in his heart every time he came home from school. And then, when he was a senior in high school, she had carried out her threat, leaving a note damning all Delaneys to hell.

Colin let the knocker drop harshly and a rosy-cheeked maid wearing a stiff black uniform and starched white apron opened the door. She was young, probably no more than sixteen, thought Della, as the girl centered a wistful smile on Colin and murmured, ''Yes?''

''We're here to see Mrs. Delaney. Mr. Colin and Miss Arnell.'' Colin deftly swept off his bowler hat and once more Della was painfully conscious of how well he seemed to fit into the manners of the time.

''Yes, sir, won't you come in, please.'' The maid stepped back and waited by the open door.

Della assumed that she was included in the invitation, even though the young woman's appreciative eyes never left Colin's face as they entered a spacious foyer filled with huge ferns and white statuary.

''Your hat, sir.''

''Thank you.'' Colin handed her his bowler and gave her a smile that made the maid's cheeks grow ruddier than ever.

Della stilled an impulse to say something sharp to him. She knew his friendliness was calculated. The maid could be a valuable source. She might be able to provide him with a wealth of intimate information about the couple and their infant son who lived in the house.

"This way, please." The young woman's ample hips moved in a saucy walk as she led them down a wide marble hall as cold as a public building corridor. The walls were stark, the dark furniture stiff and unfriendly. A circular staircase rose to a wide landing and then separated in two directions. There was no sound in the house except the loud ticking of a grandfather clock standing in the hall beside a black walnut rectory table. A silver platter placed between two silver candelabra held several calling cards left by earlier visitors.

Legitimate visitors, thought Della. *Not like us.* She shot a panicked look at Colin's determined profile. His strong resemblance to Shawn Delaney seemed more pronounced than ever. "Let's don't do this... let's go," she whispered hoarsely. "I don't like it. It doesn't feel right." She put her hand on his arm, making him stop and face her.

He looked at her as if he were miles away, in some tortured world of his own.

"Please, let's go," she begged.

"Not yet." He couldn't turn away. Not now. Even if the truth destroyed him, he had to see this through.

She started to protest but the words withered under his look of resolute determination. He wasn't going to let go. Not now... perhaps not ever. The whole situation was beyond understanding. And it broke her heart to see the pain in his eyes. She didn't know what to say or do to help. Maybe he was right. Maybe this visit would be a catharsis for him. "All right," she said as she gave him a supportive nod, "I'm with you."

He flashed her a grateful look and took a deep breath. "Let me do the talking."

The maid looked puzzled as she waited in front of a wide archway leading into a formal drawing room. She shifted her weight, putting a hand on one hip in a provocative manner. "Pardon me, sir. Shall I announce you?"

Once again, Della was struck by the maid's familiar manner. It had a touch of insolence about it. As if she was sure of her job. Curious, Della wondered if Shawn Delaney might have something to do with the maid's cavalier attitude.

Colin put a guiding hand on Della's elbow as they followed the maid into a room filled with dark furniture, heavy wall hangings and fringed velvet draperies. Thick rugs scattered on the floor muffled their footsteps and added to the somber atmosphere.

A woman sat in a straight-backed chair at the far end of the long room, reading the Bible. Her manner and stiff posture matched the gloomy, colorless room.

Colin's great-grandmother. Della felt Colin stiffen and her mouth went dry. As they approached her, Mrs. Delaney remained seated and purposely put a ribbon marker in her Bible before she set it down on the small table beside her chair. Her controlled expression never changed.

"Mr. Colin to see you," the maid announced, ignoring Della's presence once again.

"And Miss Arnell," Colin supplied quickly.

Edith Delaney gave a slight nod and with a wave of her slender hand gave them permission to be seated on a pair of hard-backed chairs opposite her. She wore a high-necked gray summer dress with a small pearl brooch as her only adornment. Not unattractive, she had balanced features and light brown hair pulled back from a high forehead. A hard cast to her blue eyes and the rigid set of her mouth gave her a brittle expression. She was somewhere in her thirties, Della guessed. She couldn't picture this woman married to the outgoing, hand-shaking man she had met in front of the hotel that morning.

"That will be all, Sally."

"Yes, ma'am." The maid gave Colin a fleeting smile as she turned and left the room.

Mrs. Delaney folded her hands in her lap and waited for Colin to speak. She gave no indication that she saw any resemblance between Colin and her husband. Maybe I'm the only one who sees it, thought Della. Maybe Colin appeared differently to everyone else.

"It's a pleasure to meet you, Mrs. Delaney," Colin said with only a trace of suppressed emotion in his voice.

Della's heartbeat quickened. What was he going to say to her? Could he control all his pent-up emotion about the Delaney family's ugly secrets?

"Thank you for seeing us," he added smoothly. "I feel that we have a lot in common."

If you only knew how much! Della thought with a hidden ironic smile. Colin was sitting across from his great-grandmother, acting for all the world as if his visit were an ordinary happening instead of the most bizarre situation anyone could imagine.

"Your note said that you were interested in Denver's citizens' league." Edith's tone was crisp, businesslike and a trifle condescending. As she measured Colin with her eyes, her guarded expression did not change, as if she saw nothing familiar about him.

"Yes, indeed. I understand that you are the founder of the organization."

The woman's tone thawed a little. "That's correct. I decided that something must be done to correct a deplorable and disgraceful situation in our city. My husband has always been civic-minded and I feel that a wife's duty lies in helping her husband achieve his ambitions."

"Very commendable," Colin said evenly. "I'm sure the league could become a model for other communities, Mrs. Delaney." His subtle flattery had the desired effect. The woman visibly relaxed.

"I'm glad to be of help, of course." Her face lost its guarded look and became animated as she explained how the idea for the civic group had been conceived and organized.

As she talked, Della searched for some visible trait the woman might have passed on to her great-grandson, but nothing in the woman's pale coloring, faded blue eyes, and angular body matched Colin's. He was his great-grandfather through and through. Della was amazed that the woman didn't seem to notice the resemblance to her husband. *Am I the only one who sees Colin as a reproduction of Shawn Delaney?*

"I understand your husband is buying up property on Market and Larimer streets," Della said boldly, injecting herself into the conversation. Colin gave her a quick look. Surprise or irritation, she could not tell which.

The woman's probing eyes met Della's with a slight rise of an eyebrow. "Are you acquainted with my husband, Miss . . . ?"

"Arnell. I've met him," she answered evenly. *This morning. In front of my hotel.*

"I see." She made no effort to answer Della's question.

"We were wondering," Colin said, picking up the gauntlet, "why Mr. Delaney is interested in investing money in the least desirable section of Denver. I mean, the city is growing to the east and south, isn't it? Why not buy property that will have a better resale value?"

Della hid a smile. Colin was looking ahead a hundred years, knowing that the land that passed to him could have been choice lots in the center of the expanding city. The family coffers would have prospered through the years if the land Shawn Delaney had acquired had been in a different section of town.

"There are more important considerations than resale values, Mr. Colin. My husband is determined to change lower downtown Denver by buying up those properties."

"And once he owns most of Market Street, what then?" Colin's voice was edged with cynicism.

"The gambling houses and prostitution parlors will be torn down. Mr. Delaney has done all he can as a member of the city council. Somehow, the devil's work continues to go on despite fines, revoked liquor and gambling licenses and town ordinances. All efforts to legally close these places have failed."

"What if the owners refuse to sell?" Della asked. She knew that Maude Mullen would see Shawn Delaney dead before she'd give up her business.

Once again, Edith's biting gaze settled on Della. "Righteousness will prevail."

At what cost? Would Edith Delaney think her husband's life worth her crusade? Della didn't think so. There was a flicker of warmth in her eyes when Edith mentioned her husband. The woman might present a hard, unemotional exterior to the world, but Della suspected that she showed her husband a different side.

"Is it true that your husband is being considered as a gubernatorial candidate?" she asked.

Once more, there was a decided warming in her eyes. "Yes, we're confident that he will be the next Democratic governor of the state of Colorado."

Della avoided looking at her. *It's not going to happen. Someone is going to bury a knife in her husband's back.*

The woman shifted her attention to Colin. "We will be needing broad community backing. Can we depend upon your support, Mr. Colin?"

"You can be sure that I'll do what I can to keep informed of Mr. Delaney's activities," he told her, the double meaning painfully clear to Della.

Edith pointedly picked up her Bible again. "Please let me know if I can be of further assistance."

Colin stood up. "Thank you for your time." He moved to the side of her chair and looked down at his great grandmother in a way that made Della wonder for a moment if he was going to say something that would give away his relationship to her.

I am your great-grandson...from the twentieth century.

What would the woman do? Call the police? Have him locked up? Della watched a multiplicity of emotions cross Colin's face. She held her breath and her heart broke its rhythmic beating.

"I'm very glad to have met you, Mrs. Delaney. You'll never know how much it has meant to me." He looked ready to bend over and kiss his great-grandmother's forehead. After a while, he held out his hand to her.

With a quizzical frown, she gingerly put her hand in his. Edith stared up at him for a long moment, then drew her hand away, and said crisply, "Good day, Mr. Colin."

"I hope you have a happy...life. Goodbye." He swallowed, trying to hold back a flood of emotion. Then he turned to Della and said in a ragged voice, "Let's go."

They walked down the hall and had reached the front entrance hall just as a motherly nanny pushed a huge baby carriage through the front door.

"Good day, sir," the woman said, preparing to push the baby buggy past them.

"Wait a minute." Colin moved to the side of the buggy and looked down at an infant nestled in blue blankets. The tiny baby boy had dark blue eyes and a cap of raven black hair. "Ian Delaney?" he said, touching his fingers to the little fist.

The gray-haired lady nodded.

Colin's chest tightened. *My grandfather.* The realization brought a stab of pain. He had hated Ian Delaney with a consuming passion all his life. This appealing little infant holding on to Colin's finger had turned into a grasping, selfish miser who had deliberately made life hell for everyone around him. What had twisted and corroded his spirit into the cruel satyr that everyone hated? Ian had been raised without a father and looking into the infant's cherubic face, Colin wondered how different all their lives might have been if Shawn Delaney had not been stabbed on the steps of a cathouse. He didn't believe for one minute that his great-grandfather's motive for investing his money in Denver's red-light district was altruistic. Shawn Delaney's greed had not only got him murdered but had laid the seeds for the family's destruction.

Della looked from Colin to the infant who was his grandfather, and she felt her heart constrict.

"Excuse me, please, but I'd best be getting the little one upstairs," said the nanny. "Are you a friend of the family's, sir?"

Colin gave a coarse laugh and shook his head. "No. I wish I were . . . just a friend."

The nursemaid gave him a puzzled look as she quickly pushed the buggy past him and disappeared down the hall.

"Let's get out of here," Colin said gruffly. "I've had enough Delaney family history for one day."

Della anxiously studied his stony profile on the ride back to Market Street. He was lost in a dark reverie, miles away. What an ordeal, she thought with a surge of tenderness. Impulsively, she leaned over and kissed his cheek. "I'm sorry. That must have been rough."

The stony gaze in his eyes faded as he turned and looked at her. "I'm glad you were with me." He put his arm around her shoulder and she leaned back against it as the hansom cab jolted along the street.

The sky had clouded over and a soft rain began to fall. The rhythmic clatter of the horse's hooves blended with the soft patter of drops on the canvas top.

He must be going over everything that happened, thought Della. Every word. Every feeling. Lamenting what he said...or didn't say. She let her fingers lightly caress the hand holding hers. "Want to talk about it?"

He gave a weary sigh. "Maybe you were right all the time. Maybe I shouldn't have gone to the house. I thought the visit would help me straighten out some of my thinking about my family, but my emotions are more tangled than ever. I came away feeling sorry for my great-grandmother and angry with the infant who would grow up to be my grandfather. I almost put my arms around Edith Delaney and told her who I was. I wanted to prepare her for the unhappiness ahead. She must have been devastated to have her husband murdered in the part of town she had dedicated herself to changing. I wonder if she suspected that Shawn Delaney wasn't the upright politician he pretended to be?"

"I think she loved him. Under that controlled exterior of hers, I bet she's capable of deep passion. Did she ever marry again?"

"No. She raised the baby by herself and devoted herself to community work. She refused to have anything to do with the Market Street properties after Shawn's death. It all went to Ian and then to me, bypassing my father."

"Who did Ian marry? And did you know her?"

"No, I didn't...My grandfather married a young girl, seventeen years old when he was thirty-five. My

father was their only child and my grandfather outlived him." His lips tightened. "I thought that by
selling off the property that was left to me, I could rid
myself of the family's infamous past. And look what
happened! I sold the hotel to you and here we are."

"Yes, here we are," she echoed.

She stared out the side of the cab. A fluke of cir-
cumstance had brought her into Colin Delaney's life
and everything about the present situation frightened
her. How could any promise of feelings between them
be fulfilled when at any moment, he could turn his
back on her. He had asked her to trust him but how
could she trust the mounting physical attraction between them when the bizarre fate that had brought
him into her life could just as easily take him away?
She gave a silent, ragged sigh.

By the time they reached the boardinghouse, the
heavens had opened up in a steady downpour. It reminded Della of the night Colin arrived at her hotel,
drenched and dripping. A week ago—or several lifetimes?

Colin paid the driver and hurried her into the
boardinghouse instead of walking her across the alley
to Maude's place.

"I should get back to the office," Della protested
halfheartedly. "Maude will know I haven't spent all
this time at the dressmaker's."

"Relax. She and that hairy-faced Gilly are gone for
the afternoon. I heard them yelling at each other. He's
run up a bunch of debts and it sounds as if she's not
going to bail him out this time. He was making all
kinds of threats. Hell, I wish she'd let me boot him out

of the house for good," Colin swore. "I don't like the idea of him hanging around you."

"I can handle him," Della said. "Don't pick a fight with him. He's the kind that would pull out a pair of brass knuckles and smash that handsome nose of yours."

Colin raised an eyebrow. "Handsome nose? For that compliment, I'll show you my room. In fact, I have several slices of poppy seed cake hidden away." He grinned as if he'd already discovered the way to her heart was her appetite. "Trudie brought me a loaded tray last night."

"Do you think we should?"

"Why not?"

Such behavior wasn't proper in a time of bustles and crinolines, but maybe society had made some advances, she thought as she lifted her skirt and climbed the stairs beside him.

"There are mostly single guys here," Colin said as he unlocked his door. "They leave early in the morning and come back late at night. There's a line for the communal bathroom, let me tell you. I got acquainted with several while waiting my turn this morning. Well, what do you think?" He gave a sweep of his hand. "A bachelor pad, 1880s-style."

The room was clean and filled with worn but comfortable furniture, a brass bed, a small hand-hewn table, and a worn easy chair. She was surprised to see a pipe rack and a canister of pipe tobacco. "I didn't know you smoked a pipe."

"I don't, but Trudie insisted on bringing those to me. She said I reminded her of her husband who, according to her, was a fine specimen of a man who cut a dandy figure with the ladies. I guess I have a reputation to live up to," he said solemnly.

She moved away from him, too aware of the intimacy his nearness invited. "Where's the cake? Or did you get me up here under false pretenses?" she teased, trying to hide her quickening pulse.

He put a mocking hand over his heart. "You wound me to the quick. Would I lie about something as important as poppy seed cake?"

She laughed. "Never."

"Sit down, pretty lady, and I'll share my larder with you, down to the last crumb. Sorry I don't have a bottle of wine stashed away."

He went to a shelf that held a couple of books and a plate covered with a white napkin. "See, I'm a man of my word," he said as he offered her the cake.

Della took off her damp straw hat and tossed it on the floor. She then curled up in the worn easy chair and ate a thick slice of cake while Colin sat on the edge of the bed and watched her.

"If I hadn't watched you put away that huge lunch, I'd have sworn you hadn't eaten for days." He chuckled. "How do you keep a willowy figure with that bus driver's appetite?"

She shook her head. "I don't know, but I'm thankful for it."

He gave her an appreciative wink. "So am I."

The tension of the afternoon faded away. Colin played host and kept up a light train of conversation, choosing subjects that had nothing to do with the situation in which they found themselves. They talked about food and argued about music and books. She glimpsed a side of Colin that she had never suspected. He had been a shy boy living alone with an abusive mother and had somehow found the strength to rise above his wretched upbringing. He told her he liked to hike, ride bicycles, and had even entered marathon charity races for the fun of it. As an adult he had developed a great interest in jazz and he confessed that he knew all the night spots where jiving musicians hung out. Della could picture him sitting in a quiet corner, breathing in every note.

"I never had the courage to break free of my aunt's strict upbringing," she confessed. Listening to him talk about his varied interests and activities, she realized how narrow her life had become. Unlike Colin, she had retreated into work as her only outlet. "I lived in an old house with my Aunt Frances until her death. I never developed any real friends or hobbies, and I guess I just defined myself as a businesswoman," she continued. How empty all that seemed now. "I never dated much and my one affair was about as hot as lukewarm milk. That's why I was surprised when you teased me about a smoldering passion."

He looked at her with a soft, regretful smile.

"What are you thinking?" she asked, suddenly embarrassed by her honesty with him.

"Not thinking...wishing." Once the words were out, he regretted admitting the truth. Fantasizing about what might have been between him and Della was idiotic. Under these strange circumstances, he'd never make the mistake of committing himself. He had nothing to offer a woman as brave and caring as Della. She deserved the very best, and he had nothing but the moment to give her.

Della rose, came over to the bed, and sat down beside him. For an hour they'd been able to behave as if they were two people getting to know each other. "Tell me. I want to know."

"I guess I was wishing that things might have been different," he admitted, her nearness sending a pulsating arousal through him. He could feel a building desire that would soon be evident if she didn't move away. The very air between them was charged.

Her candid eyes admitted her need to draw from his strength. "We could pretend . . . couldn't we?" she asked softly.

He searched her face. "I can't promise you anything. Lord knows I wish I could but I can't. I'd only be lying."

"I know." Her body had never responded this way to a man's masculinity. A longing to be loved and caressed came from some untouched depth of emotions. Her heart started beating a little too fast and she knew what was going to happen. In a moment, there would be no turning back.

Colin reached over and slowly, purposefully, removed the large hairpins from the prim coil at the back of her head and ran his fingers through her hair until it sprang in a tangled pale softness around her face.

"Lovely," he whispered as the sensuous feel of the strands slipping through his fingers sent a quiver of pleasure through him. He cupped the back of her head and brought her lips to his. His tongue teased the sweetness of her mouth until it parted, sending a message of rising hunger as she returned his kisses.

"Your dress is damp," he murmured as his hands slipped to her breasts and deftly began to undo the tiny buttons on the tight bodice. He slipped the dress off her shoulders and let it fall to the floor.

She'd never had a man undress her before. He tossed aside each garment, creating waves and waves of pleasure as he trailed kisses over her bare shoulders and buried his lips in the sweet valley of her breasts. She shivered but not from the cool air upon her bare skin. A tantalizing flicker of his tongue on each rising nipple sent heat spiraling through her. An ache of desire brought a murmured plea to her lips. A fire of warmth compelled her to breathe his name.

Colin laid her down upon the bed, quickly discarded his own clothing and then sank beside her on the down-filled mattress. She engaged his senses like no other woman he had known, and for the first time in his life, he surrendered all of himself.

With a delight that made each caress deeper and more intimate, he explored the soft lines and curves of her body, molding her swelling breasts with his cupped hands. Burying his face in the sweet valley of her breasts, he let his lips slide over her soft skin. Her breath caught in a low moan as he kissed each nipple, flicking the rosy tips with his tongue.

She'd never known such compelling hunger and she drew him closer, letting her hands trace his muscular back and thighs. His maleness both excited and dismayed her. No wonder the meaning of life had always been defined by lovers, she thought as a building rhythm of exploding sensation joined them together.

Outside, a clap of thunder rent the sky and rain beat against the windowpane in a wild fury. Lightning darted across the sky. The air was heavy and sultry, and there was no reality beyond the passion that engulfed them. No awareness except a shared ecstasy. At the heart of their lovemaking was defiance against a fate that might dare to separate them.

Chapter 9

The sky grew light after the brief storm and turned a shimmering blue. Sunlight pouring through the window bathed the rumpled bed in a bright glow. Della pushed the hair back from her eyes. Her whole body felt indolent and wonderfully at peace. She turned and pressed her lips against Colin's bare chest and snuggled against his virile length.

The rain was over and in the street below sounds of activity grew louder and floated up into the room. They could hear jingling harnesses, groaning wheels, neighing horses and blustery drivers shouting at their horses and other drivers. The raucous sounds dispelled the blessed suspension from time and place.

Colin held her tightly and stared at the ceiling as the world intruded upon the oasis they had created for themselves. He reached for the pocket watch he'd placed on the nightstand. "Five o'clock."

She groaned. "I don't care." He smiled as she cuddled in closer. "What do you say we never leave this room and never set foot inside Maude Mullen's Pleasure House again?"

For an answer, he tugged lightly on her sensuous lips, then let his mouth trail down the sweet curve of her neck.

"I don't want to go back to the house . . . ever," she whispered as she cupped his dark head and pressed his face into her soft breasts.

They made love again, and when they heard sounds on the stairs, Colin pulled away reluctantly. "I've got to get you out of here before Trudie finds out. She laid down the law about women visitors."

Della reached for her clothes. "That seems a little hypocritical considering the fact that she told you she had retired from the business."

"I doubt if it's a moral issue. Trudie probably doesn't want a bunch of call girls running all over the house. She's a crusty old gal. Probably seen enough of base human nature to wash her hands of it for good. I rather like her, though. She's gone out of her way for me."

Della's eyes twinkled. "I bet you're the best-looking guy she's had under her roof for a long time."

"Compliments will get you everywhere," he said and took the time to kiss her again.

When Della had finished putting on the old-fashioned clothes and had managed to get her tousled hair back in its prim coil, Colin nodded his approval. "Ready?"

She lifted her face for one last kiss. "If we could walk out of this room and back into our own time and place this very minute, would you do it?"

The expression that crossed his face was answer enough.

"I'm sorry," she said quickly. "Just a rhetorical question."

"And my rhetorical answer—maybe."

He cautiously opened the bedroom door, eased his head out and looked in both directions. "Come on." He took her arm and guided her swiftly into the hall.

They made it down the stairs and out the back door of the boardinghouse without seeing anyone. Colin closed the door softly behind them and guided Della down some wooden steps.

She gave a hasty look around the backyard, surprised to see that it was filled with flowers, brick walks, velvet green grass and a large gazebo with a profusion of vines trailing over it.

"Your landlady must love gardening."

"She's always puttering around the house with fresh flowers in her hands. I suspect she might have been raised on a farm. She's always talking about Nebraska."

Colin hurried Della through a gate set in a high wooden fence. They crossed the alley to Maude's property. High weeds, rampant flower beds and a miserable kitchen garden made a sharp contrast to the yard they had just left. A stable stood behind the house, and steep steps led to living quarters above. Della guessed that Jack Gilly and Maude's son must live there.

Scowling freckled-faced Billy was in the process of unhitching a huge gray dray horse from a buckboard. The boy jerked around as Della and Colin came into the overgrown, weed-filled backyard. He immediately grabbed a whip off the wagon and sent them a threatening glare as he fingered the rawhide strip of leather.

"We must be trespassing on his territory," Della said with a shiver. The boy looked ready to lash out with the whip if they came any closer. His dark loathing rolled toward them with the ferocity of a storm cloud. She tightened the arm she had slipped through Colin's. "I wonder why he feels threatened."

"A combination of things, no doubt. Growing up can leave deep scars." His jaw tightened. "I know."

She glanced at his granitelike expression and a rising compassion mingled with the tenderness she felt for him. His mother had told him that he came from bad Delaney seed and she must have blamed her son for the wretched life she'd had with her alcoholic husband. Della shuddered to think about the deep scars the woman had left.

Colin opened the back door for her. "Stay in your room at the back of the house tonight, love. I don't want to be worrying about you."

"You're the one who needs to be cautious." She choked back the lurking fear that somehow his great-grandfather's murder was going to involve Colin. "What if Shawn Delaney shows up?"

"I hope he does," he answered curtly.

"What'll you do?"

"Try to get some answers."

"And maybe stir up trouble that you can't handle?" *What if someone mistakes you for Shawn Delaney.* "I'm frightened. This morning, you made an enemy out of Jack Gilly—"

"Only because you were involved." He put his hands lightly on her arms as they stood in the doorway. "That's why I don't want you around tonight. Promise me, you'll make yourself scarce once the entertainment starts."

"When will I see you again?"

"We'll find some time. I promise." His deep blue eyes stroked her face with a caress that pulled her to him like a grappling hook. She almost leaned into him until she glanced over his shoulder and she saw Billy still standing there with the whip in hand, glaring at them.

She pulled back. If Colin kissed her, Billy might tell Maude and she didn't know what forces would be brought into play if the woman kicked them out of the house. "Don't..." Della put a hand against Colin's chest and lightly pushed him back.

He frowned. "What—"

"Billy." She shivered. "Thank God he's got a whip in his hand instead of a gun or we both might have a bullet in our backs."

Colin swung around. "Go on about your business, Billy," he yelled at the boy.

The scowling boy didn't move.

"Now." Colin took a step toward him and Billy bolted. Still clutching the whip, the boy disappeared into the shadows of the open barn door.

Della shivered again in the bright sunshine.

"If he bothers you, let me know," Colin said, turning to her. "And now I'll take that goodbye kiss."

He pressed her back against the doorframe. His mouth caught hers, tasting, pulling and bruising her lips with a warmth that reignited the desire between them. The smoldering coals of their recent passion flared into a fierce heat. "Oh, Lord," he groaned as he reluctantly pulled away.

"That was no goodbye kiss," Della said, her own breath thick and heavy.

Colin struggled to get his emotions under control. He'd never had a woman send him into such a tailspin. At a time when he needed all his wits about him, he knew that he could never concentrate unless he knew she was safe. "I've changed my mind. I don't want you to stay here."

"What are you talking about? You kept telling me we had no choice."

"*I'm* the one who doesn't have a choice. We have to find someplace where you'll be safe."

"And you'll go with me? Leave this house... and Market Street?" She set her mouth in a firm line. "I'm not going anywhere unless you go, too."

"Don't be so blasted stubborn."

"Would you define that word for me?" she snapped. "Stubborn as in obstinate, bullheaded or obsessed?"

They glared at each other. The physical and sexual arousal between them had found a different outlet. Anger afforded them a refuge from the torment of wanting too much. She jutted out her chin. "Don't try to manipulate me. If we leave... we leave together."

He gave her one of his dark, unfathomable looks. "All right. If that's the way you want it." He turned away and strode down the alley toward the front of the house.

She opened her mouth to call him back and then closed it. She blinked away hot tears of frustration, and a sense of utter loneliness settled on her as she went down the back hall to Vinetta's room.

She lay down on the bed and let the day's events wash over her. Since that morning, she had been battered with enough emotion to fill a lifetime. No, not one lifetime. *Two* lifetimes. The past and the present, interwoven. And that's what frightened her. The same day that she had met Shawn Delaney, she'd made love with his great-grandson who was almost the same age. Colin's grandfather had been an infant in a baby buggy and Colin had held his tiny hand. In twenty-four hours, she had experienced two different threads of time. What if the threads of past lives became snagged and knotted with those to be lived a hundred years later?

She closed her eyes against a mounting headache. How could it be that she'd found someone who could make her feel totally alive, only to be faced with losing him? Because of Colin she had discovered a sensual part of herself she never knew existed. She'd always shied away from loving or trusting people and somewhere she'd picked up the idea that it wasn't in her makeup to care for any man. But Colin was dangerously close to leveling all her preconceived ideas. He had shown her that she was capable of passion, and had allowed her to give herself wholly and completely. His strength of character challenged her intellectually and emotionally. Heaven help her if she fell in love with him. If only they weren't trapped in a time not their own. If only... As if to mock her thoughts, a faint scent of lilacs touched her nostrils.

Della stiffened. "I don't want your blasted job or room," she said to the empty room. "Show me the way and I'll leave!" She waited. The lilac scent faded and only the muffled sounds that came from the rest of the house broke the stillness.

She flounced over on her pillow and let warm tears ease down her cheeks. There had to be a way to escape these historical events without being drawn into them. Her thoughts floundered in every direction until a bone-weariness overtook her and she let herself slip into a numbing sleep.

When she awoke a couple of hours later, the room was in shadowy darkness. She turned on a small lamp with a ruffled shade, then opened the door and stepped into the hall. A frantic party-time bustle from the kitchen greeted her ears.

Above the clatter, she could hear Inga's strident orders cursing the help. "Stupid fool! Don't overload those trays! Make two trips! Cut that bread thinner!"

Cooking and baking smells reminded her that it had been a long time since her feast at Delmonte's. She cautiously eased down the hall and peered through the door into the kitchen. Platters of food were being carried out of the room, accompanied by champagne buckets filled with chopped ice. Maude might stint on her employees' fare, thought Della, but the madam put on elaborate cuisine for her male guests, and at a good profit as the books had shown.

Della stopped at a worktable where Lolly was making roast beef sandwiches and helped herself to one. The girl's eyes widened and she sent a scared glance at Inga. The broad-shouldered cook had her back to them at the moment.

Della gave Lolly a reassuring smile and moved on to help herself to a couple of pastries oozing with apricot preserves. Della made her way around the bustling kitchen and sampled any food she could pick up with her fingers.

When Inga finally realized she had an unwelcome scavenger in her domain, she ordered her out, then told her, "Lolly will bring you a tray when it's time."

"Don't bother." Della bit into a stuffed cabbage roll that she had lifted from one of the plates. "The amount of food you put on my tray isn't worth Lolly's shoe leather. I'll just serve myself . . . save you the trouble."

Inga's double chin quivered. "I'll be telling Miss Maude about this."

"Please do. And while you're at it, tell her I'd like my tea hot from now on." Della swallowed the last of the roll and licked her fingers. "Delicious. You're a marvelous cook, Inga. Maude's lucky to have you."

The compliment took a little of the sting out of Inga's "Hmmph, stay out of my kitchen."

Maude's office door was open but the madam wasn't at her desk. Thank heavens, thought Della. She was probably in for a tongue blistering for having disappeared all afternoon, but the memory of the hours spent in Colin's arms made any tongue-lashing well worth it.

She had just sat down at her desk, when a teenage girl clutching a large canvas bag appeared in the doorway. She hesitated and looked for a moment as if she was going to turn around and flee. Her face was plain and she wore an unbecoming navy dress and black shoes. Her brown hair was stuck under a plain wide-brimmed hat.

"Can I help you?" Della asked quickly. The girl couldn't be more than sixteen, she thought. *A prospective boarder?* Della walked around her desk, calculating how she could turn her away before Maude got her hands on the teenager.

"Please excuse me," the girl said with a quick subservient dip as if she'd been trained to curtsy before her elders. "Are you...Maude Mullen?"

Della knew she must have blanched. "No. I'm her secretary...I mean, bookkeeper."

"Oh?" The girl hesitated and clutched the handle of her portmanteau.

"She's probably busy right now. Maybe I can help. Why don't you come in and sit down."

Her eyes skittered over Della. "Thank you, ma'am, but I came to see someone...if that's all right. I mean, I was told to ask..." Her voice trailed off.

"Who is it you want to see?"

"Lilyanne." Her eyes were round with fear. "I know she's here."

"Yes, of course she's here," Della answered in surprise. Was Lilyanne going to get the girl a place in the house? "Did she tell you to come to see about... work?"

"Oh, no, ma'am. I already have a place."

Della sighed. The girl was already attached to another house. "Well, I'm glad to meet a friend of Lilyanne's. She's a very nice person."

"Can I see her...I mean...would it be all right? I wouldn't get into trouble, would I?" She looked at Della like a scared rabbit peeping out of a hole. "I've never been in a place like this before."

"You haven't? Then you don't work in a house like this?"

The girl gave a quick shake of her head. "No, miss."

"What is your name?" Della asked gently.

"Jenny."

"Well, Jenny, I'm sure that Lilyanne will be glad for company. Go up the stairs to the third floor and down the hall to the last door on your right. You may even hear Lilyanne singing before you get there."

"She always was one for singing to keep her spirits up." The girl's plain face lightened with a hint of a smile.

"Have you known her for a long time?"

Jenny nodded and turned away. "Thank you very much," she said over her shoulder as she scurried out into the hall.

Della stared after her, puzzled. She made a mental note to ask Lilyanne about her as she walked to her desk and sat down once more.

Maude had left a scribbled message on Della's desk. "A dressmaker's fitting does *not* mean a free afternoon." The word *not* was underlined several times. "You owe me six hours work! Tonight!"

A stack of correspondence was piled high. Maude had scribbled her answer on each letter in the stack, mostly orders for supplies or inquiries about late orders. It took Della over two hours to type answers on an old iron typewriter. To someone conditioned to the age of computers, the task was totally frustrating and time-consuming.

By the time she had finished, she could tell from the sounds bouncing off the walls that the night's entertainment was in full swing. Piano and violin music swelled above the din of laughter and voices. She was surprised to hear familiar songs like "There's a Tavern in the Town" and "The Sidewalks of New York." She heard a baritone singing "I'll Take You Home Again, Kathleen." Her eyes misted as she felt a surge of longing for her handsome Irishman. *Colin...Colin.*

The longing was so painful that she got to her feet and restlessly walked around the room. She couldn't play a waiting game. She had to do something, anything, that might offer a way to escape back into the time period where they belonged. What about the tunnel? Colin said he had checked for it. How thoroughly?

She hesitated and then made a decision. They had come into this time warp through a tunnel. All things being logical—which God knows they weren't—they should be able to return through the same passage.

Della left the office just as Lolly came by on her way to the kitchen with some empty glasses. "Where's the basement?" Della asked.

The girl blinked without answering.

"The basement. You know... cellar? Under the house?"

"Oh, yes'um." Lolly nodded with understanding, then shook her dark curly head. "Don't like it." She backed up as if Della was about to send her there. "Don't like it."

"It's all right, Lolly. I want to look for something. Where are the cellar steps? Will you show me? You don't have to go down."

The young girl seemed unconvinced but she reluctantly led the way to a scullery off the kitchen. She pointed to a closed wooden door and then scurried off before Della had a chance to thank her.

If fancy women were going from the house, through a tunnel, to the hotel across the street, there should be some sign of traffic, reasoned Della, but only an empty darkness yawned at Della as she opened the cellar door. The walls were bare dirt and rock, and narrow steps disappeared into the blackness below.

Della stood on the landing and looked around for a light switch. When she spied a gray string hanging down from above, she gave it a jerk. A bare light bulb sent a circle of pale yellow light upon the stairs. Carefully, she descended the warped wooden stairs, cursing her long skirt that threatened to trip her with every step. A dank earth smell came up to greet her and she could see why Lolly didn't like going down into the crudely dug space.

When she reached the bottom, she stood for a long moment, her eyes adjusting to the murky darkness. Finally, she made out a jumble of discarded household objects—broken chairs, blackened pans, chipped dishes and several old trunks.

A wooden bin filled with coal had a chute leading to the outside and she could see where someone had left a shovel, probably after filling coal buckets for the numerous fireplaces. A faint odor of tobacco touched her nostrils. Cigar? Pipe? Someone must have been down here smoking. Maybe Billy, she thought, suddenly uneasy. She wouldn't want to run into him in an isolated place like this.

Holding up her skirt, she walked around the perimeter of the cellar as best she could. In several spots she couldn't get close enough to the wall to examine it, but in the dim light she couldn't see any sign of a tunnel leading from the cellar to the hotel across the street. It seemed unlikely that any elaborately dressed young women had made their way across the street from this cold, bleak hole in the ground.

She mentally went over all the possibilities. The tunnel had existed and had been closed off for years when her workmen found it. The phantom ladies that had invaded her hotel matched those living in Maude's house, but Della didn't know if she and Colin had arrived before or after the tunnel had been in use. She only knew that the passageway had swept them back in time and was the only clue she had for trying to secure a return trip to the twentieth century.

Disappointed in her failure to find anything resembling a tunnel, she started up the stairs. She had almost reached the top, when a man's bulk filled the doorway.

"Well, I'll be damned. What in the hell?" Jack Gilly swore in surprise. "Maudie's little uppity biddy. Snooping around for my hidden booze, I'll wager." He reached out, grabbed her roughly by the arms and pulled her up the last two steps and into the scullery.

"Take your hands off me!"

"She put you up to it, didn't she? A man can't even have himself a bottle around this blasted place."

"I don't know anything about your bottle... and could care less! Let go of me."

"Then what you doing down them stairs?"

"None of your business." She jerked free and took a couple of steps before he grabbed her again.

"I'm making it my business," he snarled. "There's something smelly going on here. You and that smart-mouthed dandy don't have me fooled none."

"I don't know what you're talking about," she gasped, unable to break the hold his thick hands had on her. His rancid breath mingled with the strong odor of a cigar stuck in his coat pocket.

"I'm warning you. Nobody's moving in on me or Maude, got that?" He put his sour-smelling face close to hers and his moist lips spread in a leer.

"Take your hands off me!"

His mouth pulled back over yellowed teeth. "I like breaking in a high-stepping filly." His beard scraped her face as he tried to kiss her.

"No." She jerked her head to one side.

He gave a short laugh and was about to force his mouth onto hers, when a voice in the scullery doorway stopped him.

"That's enough! Let her go, Jack. You know we don't have none of that going on in this part of the house." Inga stood there with a frying pan in her hand. "You better move your booze someplace else. It don't fool me none, you sneaking down the cellar all the time for bottles you've lifted from the supply wagons."

"T'ain't none of your blasted business," Jack snarled.

"Everything that goes on at this end of the house is my business. Now, git."

Jack spat something foul and gave Della a vicious shove that almost sent her off her feet. He left by the scullery's outside door and slammed it after him.

Della just stood there, leaning against the wall, trying to catch her breath. She rubbed her wrists where Jack had bruised them.

"Don't know why Maude puts up with him. I'll be damned what she sees in the potbellied old lush." She gave a disgusted snort. "Trouble, that's all he is. Someday he's really going to put a noose around Maude's neck."

"Thanks for intervening. I—"

"I don't like snoops." Inga shook the frying pan at her. "You've been overstepping yourself all day. What you doing down the cellar?"

"I was looking . . . for something?"

"What?"

Della decided to gamble. "A tunnel?"

Inga's eyes widened. Her mouth stayed open. She stared at Della.

"I said I was in the cellar looking for a tunnel."

Inga clamped down on her jaw. "Well, you won't find nothing like that in this house."

"Are you sure?" The woman's reaction had been too pointed. "Maybe there's a tunnel and you don't know about it?" Della challenged, hoping the woman's pride would make her volunteer something, but Inga didn't rise to the bait.

"You better tend to your own business," she warned. "Poking your nose where it don't belong isn't healthy."

"Sometimes there isn't a choice." Della fixed her eyes on the woman's scowling face and said evenly, "I know there's a tunnel." *Because that's how I got here.*

Inga gave a toss of her head. "I don't know what you're talking about and I'm not wasting any more time on such nonsense. Take my advice. Keep your nose buried in Maude's books or someone may cut it off." The cook turned on her heels and disappeared into the kitchen.

Della stared after her. *She's lying. She knows something about the tunnel.*

Chapter 10

That night, Della dreamed about the tunnel. She was alone, walking slowly through the narrow passage as moonlight from some mysterious source threw filtered light on the path ahead of her. No sound, no movement of air. She couldn't hear her footsteps on the uneven ground nor the labored sound of her breathing as she wearily put one foot in front of the other. An absolute silence enveloped her as she walked and walked. The tunnel seemed endless, when suddenly she wasn't alone anymore.

Colin was ahead of her.

Even in the dim light of the passage, she could see dark hair curling on his neck and the familiar breadth of his shoulders as he walked ahead of her. She started running, trying to overtake him. *Colin...Colin...don't leave me.* But no matter how fast she ran, gasping for breath, he always stayed the same distance ahead. She called his name but no sound came out. He was about to disappear into a bright light at the end of the tunnel, when suddenly he stopped.

Grateful whimpers caught in her throat as she rushed forward. She grabbed his arm and he turned around.

She screamed.

Shawn Delaney stared at her with glassy eyes, his chest covered with blood spilling from a knife stuck in his chest.

Della's scream vibrated in her ears as she sat up in bed. Trembling, she pressed her hands against her mouth to muffle the cries lurching into her throat. The horrible dream had been so real that she felt sick to her stomach.

The pearly light of early dawn was coming through the windows as she threw back the covers. She had stayed awake until after two in the morning, listening and waiting for Colin. Finally, she had fallen asleep, only to be awakened by the nightmare.

When she passed Inga's door on her way to the bathroom, she held her breath. She was worried that her scream might have awakened the woman. Thank heavens the door stayed shut. She wasn't up to explaining why she'd had a dream about a murder that hadn't yet happened.

When she returned to her room, she knew she'd never get back to sleep. *I have to talk to Colin.* Once again, she went through Vinetta's wardrobe, braced for an onslaught of eerie disapproval, but the room remained free of the insidious lilac perfume. Maybe her imagination had conjured up the woman's hostile spirit, after all, she thought as she selected a navy skirt and white dimity blouse with leg-of-mutton sleeves and a high neckline, exactly like the one Miss Turnball was making for her. Apparently, Maude had also dictated Vinetta's attire and undoubtedly had subtracted the cost from her wages the way she did all the other girls. Why didn't they unite and insist upon choosing their own wardrobes, fumed Della, knowing full well that the power of unions lay fifty years in the future.

She quickly pinned a coil of blond hair on the top of her head and slipped quietly down the hall to the kitchen. She would have given anything for an electric coffeemaker, or at the very least some instant coffee, she thought as she looked around the kitchen. A fire in the mammoth coal range had been banked and red coals would probably ignite kindling into a cooking fire, but what if she put the darn thing out trying to heat up a teakettle? Della decided she wasn't courageous enough to incur Inga's wrath. She settled for a glass of cool milk from the ice chest.

She left the kitchen and walked down the hall toward the front door where a small light still burned in the foyer. Through the open front door, she saw that in the predawn darkness, the hotel across the street was dimly lit and the street was empty. No sign of life anywhere.

Sighing, Della closed the door and was heading back down the hall toward the office when she heard the front door open. She turned around and saw two of Maude's boarders slip into the house. A dark-haired woman in a red satin dress and a plump buxom blonde in ruffled pink organza crossed the entrance hall, lifted their skirts and hurried quietly up the stairs. A heavy perfume lingered as they passed.

Standing in the shadow of the hall, Della stiffened. Her nails bit into her palms. Was it happening again? Was she hallucinating? She walked to the foot of the stairs and as she stared upward, heard the muffled sound of a door closing. No, she wasn't imagining this. The women were real, not phantoms.

She turned around slowly. Something wasn't right. Maude's girls worked in her house, not out in the streets. Where had these two been? When she had stood at the door a couple of minutes earlier, the street had been empty. If the two women had been coming from the hotel, she would have seen them . . . *unless they had used a tunnel to return to the house.*

Her mind was suddenly swimming with new speculation. She had been looking for the tunnel inside the house. The opening must be nearby, outside.

Her heart was beating rapidly as she walked out the front door and down the five front steps. She turned around and stood in the middle of the sidewalk, staring at the house. A narrow porch skirted three sides of the house with two bay windows on each side of the door. Nothing at the front of the house indicated an opening to an underground passage.

Soft shafts of early-morning light shot across the sky as she walked around the outside of the house searching for anything that might serve as an entrance to a tunnel. She looked behind bushes, under windows, and searched the sides of the house for any hidden doors. Nothing. She returned to the front of the house, disappointed and discouraged.

Sitting down on the front steps, she watched the sunrise turn fluffy clouds an ice-cream pink and then fade into the bright light of morning. A wagon rumbled down the alley between Maude's house and the boardinghouse. All the windows at Maude's remained dark and opaque but she saw a few lights come on next door.

Impulsively, she got to her feet and walked down the sidewalk until she was in front of the boardinghouse. Bending back her head, she looked at the second-floor front window. Dark, no sign of light. Was Colin still asleep? Was he even there? She swallowed back instant panic. Her fear that he would disappear forever surfaced once more.

Driven by a compelling need for reassurance, Della walked up to the front door of the boardinghouse. She wanted to be with him. An aching loneliness mocked the lie she'd been telling herself for years—that she didn't need a man in her life. Yesterday's lovemaking had changed her forever. She didn't think she could bear it if a malicious fate snatched him away from her.

She started to knock and then drew back her hand. What legitimate reason could she possibly give for wanting to go to Colin's room? Maybe she would be lucky and could slip upstairs without being seen.

Turning the doorknob, she pushed open the door and cautiously stepped inside, listening. Muted kitchen sounds came from the back of the house. No activity in the front hall or parlor, no sounds of movement on the floor above. She took a step toward the stairs and then stopped, aware that someone had just stepped through a doorway a few steps down the center hall.

"Where do you think you're headed?" challenged a small, bony woman with dark eyes and dyed hair of uncertain reddish yellow. "Trying to slip by me, were you?"

Della stammered. "No...yes...I mean..."

The woman snorted. "Well, I'll be damned. Aiming to work my house under my nose, were you?"

Della stared at the woman she assumed was Gertrude Katz, landlady of the establishment. "What?"

"You heard me." The landlady's sharp eyes fastened on the white pleated blouse and dark walking skirt Della was wearing. One of the landlady's eyebrows lifted in surprise. "That looks like one of Vinetta's outfits."

Della nodded. "Yes, it is. I borrowed some of her things. Maude said it was okay."

"Well, I'll be." The bright-eyed woman cackled. "Now I know who you are. Maudie was telling me she'd hired a new bookkeeper. And that fellow on the second floor, Colin, was talking about you. Della...Della something or other, he said your name was. Could tell right away he was sweet on you." She held out a gnarled hand and gave Della a smile that had two bottom teeth missing. "Trudie Katz. Come on into the kitchen, I can't stand chatting out here in the hall when there's breakfast to be fixed for my working men. Vinnie used to slip over here when she could and help herself to some buttered biscuits and my crab-apple preserves." She winked at Della. "But she never let Inga know."

The spry little woman led the way into a kitchen about half the size of Maude's and, in Della's opinion, a hundred times more friendly. "That's Horace,'' Trudie said, nodding toward a bald-headed man flipping pancakes in an iron skillet.

He gave Della a quick nod and then went back to his cooking. He had bowed legs and looked as if he should be hunkered down over some campfire, thought Della. He was cooking in his undershirt, a pair of mended brown nankeen pants and dusty cowboy boots.

"Horace is the best cook west of Chicago," Trudie said with undisguised affection. She motioned to a kitchen chair painted bright yellow. "Have a seat." She poured Della a cup of boiled coffee that looked strong enough to eat the glaze off the cup. "Biscuits will be out of the oven in a couple of shakes. Tell me, how's Maudie's house doing these days? She still having trouble keeping her liquor license?''

Della smiled silently. Obviously, Trudie traded coffee and biscuits for a little inside gossip. Vinetta must have kept Trudie up-to-date on the happenings next door. Della remembered that Colin had said his landlady had been in the business at one time. Had she and Maude been rivals?

"I really don't know," Della answered honestly. "This is only my second day." *And another lifetime.*

"You met that good-for-nothing Jack Gilly yet?" Trudie asked as she bustled around the kitchen, tending to bacon on the stove and whipping eggs in a huge bowl. Della's disgusted expression made Trudie snort, "I thought so. Don't know why she doesn't kick his big fat butt out the door and be done with it. Maude's got her head on square except for that guy."

"Is Billy their son?''

She shrugged. "Maude never said. He's a mean one, that kid. In another year or two, he'll be raising hell with Maude's girls. When I had my house, I never put up with freeloaders. Had my hands full, dealing with my boarders, I did. A moody bunch, most of the girls, drank too much and loved their opium. Don't know why a gal chooses the business if she doesn't have a stomach for it." She shrugged. "A lot of them died too damn young but I guess everyone makes her own grave to lie in."

Della stared into the black coffee and thought about her sister who had been caught in the same destructive patterns over a hundred years later. *If only I had done something more to help her. Like what?* asked a reasonable inner voice. *She was as stubborn as you are.*

Trudie bustled over to the table. "Here you are...biscuits and freshly churned butter. Won't find none better. Horace used to run a chuck wagon for a big spread in North Park. My boarders never complain about the grub."

"I know. Colin likes the food...and his room." She felt warmth seeping into her cheeks. Could Trudie tell from a rumpled bed what had gone on in his room yesterday?

Trudie eyed her and then shook a bony finger. "Watch out, girl. One thing I've learned in sixty years of handling men is that not a blasted one of them can be trusted."

She turned her back on Della and gave her attention to loading up trays, which she carried out of the kitchen to a large dining room. Della had finished her biscuits, when they heard heavy footsteps on the stairs and the rumble of men's voices coming from the dining room.

"The herd is lining up at the trough," Trudie said, grabbing a couple of bowls of scrambled eggs. "Better feed them before they stampede." She turned to Della. "Want to carry those biscuits in for me?" Without waiting for Della's response, she handed her the tray and swished out of the kitchen. Her scratchy voice rose above the din as she said good morning to the men.

Della worried her lower lip as she held the tray and wondered what she should do. Maybe she should slip out the back door and make her escape? Or she could walk into that dining room and see what happened. How would Colin react when he saw her? Pleased? Or would he be angry? *Maybe he wasn't even here!* She tightened her grip on the tray and marched into the dining room.

Sitting at the far end of the table, Colin was talking to the man next to him. He didn't see Della come in.

"Hey, hey, Trudie, what we got here?" smirked a red-faced guy in overalls as Della set the tray on the table beside him. "Dessert?"

Another man's broad hand reached out and grabbed her arm. "I'll have a helping, honey."

"Send her down here," roared a bearded young fellow. "I'd like some sugar, Sugar."

"Shut up, you miserable hyenas," ordered Trudie as a wave of hooting and laughter rippled down the table.

When Colin turned to see what was causing the commotion, his dark eyes widened and the cords in his neck tightened. "What in the h—" He shoved back his chair.

Della sent him a flustered smile, turned on her heels and sped back to the kitchen.

"Hey, Colin. Down, boy."

"No fair, I saw her first."

A barrage of laughter and ribald taunts followed Colin as he left the dining room. Della took one look at his furious expression and put a kitchen chair between them. He looked ready to wring her neck.

"Good morning," she said hopefully, trying to defuse the situation.

"What in the blazes do you think you're doing?" he growled.

"Helping Trudie."

"Isn't one job enough?" He knew his tone was only making things worse but he couldn't help it. When he'd seen the men ogling and making cheap remarks about her, he wanted to knock everyone of them off their chairs. "What in the hell is going on?"

Della glanced at Horace who was leaning back against a work counter, taking in the exchange with frank curiosity. "Let's talk outside," she said.

They went down the back stairs into Trudie's garden. The fresh smell of early morning was on the dew-laden leaves and sparkling blades of grass. A couple of robins were bobbing about in one corner of the yard, looking for breakfast. Della led the way to a small bench under one of the tall maple trees.

"Now we can talk," she said in a reasonable tone as she sat down. She motioned for him to sit beside her but he remained standing.

"All right. I'm listening," he snapped. The shock of seeing her in Trudie's dining room still smarted. He had thought she was safely next door. Didn't she realize how dangerous it was for her to be wandering around, exposing herself to all kinds of uncertainties? "I want to know what you're doing here."

"I had a terrible nightmare. I had to make sure that you were all right."

Her lips quivered and his anger instantly dissipated. The worry and concern in her gray-green eyes shamed him. He should have known that when they weren't together, she was as uneasy about him as he was about her. He sat down beside her and drew her close. She closed her eyes and he lightly kissed her eyelids. "I'm sorry...I shouldn't have reacted the way I did," he murmured. "But it is stupid for you to take an extra job with Trudie so you can keep track of me."

"Oh, I'm not working for Trudie." She laughed softly. "Thanks but no thanks. I got up early this morning and had decided to make certain you were safely in your room when she caught me trying to slip upstairs."

He felt a quiver of warm desire just thinking about what would have happened if she had been successful. Then his sensible side made him scold her, "Not a good idea. There are too many men running around. And Trudie might have pulled you back down the stairs by your hair."

"The fact that I was wearing one of Vinetta's outfits seemed to instantly make me a friend. I was floored when she invited me into the kitchen for coffee and biscuits, but my empty stomach made me more than willing to accept the offer. Besides, I was glad to have a chance to talk with her. From what I can gather, Trudie and Vinetta must have exchanged gossip on a regular basis. Trudie tried to pump me about what was going on next door. I think she and Vinetta had something going in the snitching department. Maude would probably be furious if she knew how much Trudie knew about her private affairs.''

"Well, don't put yourself in the middle of it," he warned. "I don't see how what went on with Trudie and Vinetta affects us," he said with more conviction than he felt. "Just do your bookkeeping job and ignore everything else."

"That's hardly possible, given the circumstances," she countered stubbornly. "Sticking my head in the sand isn't going to change anything. I'm involved whether I want to be or not."

He wanted to argue but he knew she was right. Whatever was going on between Maude and Trudie could put Della right in the middle of the two women. One more thing to worry about. He wished he could keep her with him all the time but that was impossible.

Last night, he'd had his hands full just trying to keep himself all in one piece. One of Maude's sloe-eyed blondes had deliberately played one man against the other until both of them were like enraged bulls. Colin had had to convince one of them to bide his time with another girl. Then, when two drunks took their quarrel outside and were ready to kill each other with drawn knives, Colin had intervened and nearly got himself sliced up in the process. Maude had warned him not to call the police under any condition. "We don't want them snooping around here. Just make sure nobody gets hurt." Apparently, the admonition only included customers and not her hired help, Colin decided by the time he had risked life and limb a half-dozen times in one night.

When he got off work last night, he was beat. He had wanted more than anything to be with Della but had consoled himself as he fell into bed for three hours' sleep that she was safely ensconced in her own little room next door. He could tell from the stubborn jut of her chin that his efforts to put her in some kind a protective cocoon were hopeless.

He didn't like the way her forehead creased as if her sharp mind was working on all cylinders. "What are you thinking about?"

"I saw a couple of Maude's girls slipping into the house this morning. They must have been out turning some tricks, but I didn't see them on the street anywhere. I thought at first that there might be an entrance to the tunnel somewhere on the outside of the house instead of in the cellar but I couldn't find one. I went over every inch of the outside of that house."

He didn't trust himself to speak for a moment. No telling what danger she could bring upon herself snooping around like that. He swallowed back a sharp order for her stay inside and leave the hunting to him. She wouldn't listen. Della Arnell wasn't the kind of woman who would take orders from him or anyone else.

He slipped his arm around her shoulders and lightly kissed the soft spot behind her ear. He was learning that a gentle touch was more persuasive than a commanding tone. "I've missed you. I wish you would have made it up to my room," he murmured. "It seems like forever since yesterday."

"I thought you might pay me a visit last night," she answered as she turned and caught a kiss on her lips.

"I wanted to but I had to stay on the job until nearly two. Besides, I was afraid to risk it. You know what Maude said. She'd turn you out in the street if she caught me in your room."

"Maybe it would be better if—" She broke off. Her eyes widened. Trudie stood in the doorway, glaring at them.

"What is it?" he asked.

Della nodded toward the boardinghouse.

Trudie let the screen door slam behind her as she came stomping down the wooden steps. She marched over to them, her eyes snapping. "Out! Both of you. Right now. This is my private yard. You're trespassing."

"I'm sorry, Trudie..."

"I told you when you moved in, Colin, that nobody uses the backyard without my permission. I have to let a bunch of clumsy, loud-talking male boarders have the run of the house, but the backyard is mine! Understand?"

"Sorry, Trudie," Colin said smoothly, getting to his feet and lending a hand to Della. "We didn't intend to offend you."

"I quit the business because I was tired of not having any privacy. Never could get away by myself. Now, I can." She shook a bony finger at them. "You can find someplace else to do your sparkin'."

"We won't intrude upon your privacy again," Colin promised.

"See that you don't."

"Your flower gardens are lovely, Trudie. My Aunt Frances never could get her begonias to bloom like that," Della said, and was rewarded by a slight easing of the landlady's pursed lips. "You certainly put Maude's yard to shame."

"If she'd put those lazy menfolk to work, she could have something besides weeds growing a foot tall," she snapped as she opened the side gate. "You can go out this way."

"Thank you," Della said, pretending that she didn't know the gate existed even though yesterday they had slipped out of the yard that way after their rendezvous in Colin's room. They heard Trudie latch the gate behind them.

Colin frowned as they walked down the alley to the front of Maude's house. "That's odd. Trudie acts as if she keeps the backyard for herself, but I'm positive I heard someone out there with her the first night we were here. I wonder if she has a gentleman friend we don't know about."

Chapter 11

A somnolent air still lay on the house when they entered the front hall. Colin quickly drew Della into the shadows of the front parlor and kissed her with a pent-up hunger that was at once tender, urgent and demanding. He knew that his feelings for her were sabotaging his efforts to keep a clear head but he couldn't put aside his deep possessive feelings. He'd lost his temper in a split second that morning when he saw that she was the center of lustful, leering looks and bawdy remarks.

He silently cursed himself for getting emotionally entangled. It wasn't fair to Della. His obsession with Shawn Delaney made it impossible to turn away from this chance to free himself of the hated man's shadow. His tortured spirit was not free to claim the love she offered. He would never want her to be entangled in the dark pattern of his family's history.

"What am I going to do about you?" he murmured, kissing her and letting his hands trace the sweetness of her face. Her body slackened against him. He knew that in another moment they would be caught in a swell of unbridled desire. *This is not the time. Nor the place.* Any minute, someone in the house could intrude upon them. Risking Maude's reaction was too big a gamble. Whether he liked it or not, they had to follow the rules the madam had set. He let his hands drop away from Della's face and lifted his mouth from her warm, soft lips. Then he put his hands on her shoulders and set her away from him.

She gave a breathless sigh and a weak smile. They could hear kitchen sounds beginning to float down the hall.

"I guess I'd better go," she said.

He nodded but neither of them moved.

"How did last night go?" she asked, stalling.

He shrugged. "I broke up a couple of fights and escorted a few rowdy drunks out the door. Nothing I couldn't handle."

He had probably been in more danger of getting hurt than he was admitting, she thought with a familiar quiver of anxiety. "What are you going to do today?" she asked.

"Everything from running a dozen errands to laying new carpet in one of the parlor rooms."

"You're not going to go back to the Delaney house, are you?" She was ashamed of the way her heart suddenly started pounding.

"I have no desire to go back there. I've seen my great-grandmother and my hopes of connecting with her on some personal level were just wishful thinking."

"What about your great-grandfather?"

"What about him?" His face was grim.

"You've met all the other members of your family. When are you going to contact Shawn Delaney?"

"This afternoon."

"This afternoon?" she echoed, startled. "Where?"

"Here." She saw the muscles in his cheeks tense. "He sent word to Maude last night that he's coming around to see her about three o'clock."

"No, don't let him come. You should warn him to stay away from here."

"I thought you already did that when you met him. Didn't you tell me that he brushed aside the warning?" Colin's mouth was drawn in a tight line. "Do you think he'd pay any attention to me?"

Della's chest tightened. Colin was right. Shawn Delaney wasn't going to listen to anyone. "Are you going to confront him?"

Colin's hands tightened at his side. "Maude wants me to be ready to throw him out. I told her I'd be happy to oblige." A cold rage built behind his eyes. "I've been looking forward to getting my hands on the bastard."

"Colin! Don't do it!" she begged. "Don't get involved. Learning the truth about him is one thing but you're not going to change anything by jeopardizing your own life. All your pent-up anger about what he was—or is—has already been set in time. He's going to be killed, we know that—" She broke off as a paralyzing thought leapt to the front of her mind.

"What is it?"

"No," she gasped and stepped back. *Was it possible that Colin had been brought back in time to do the murderous deed?* Could his obsession about his dark heredity have brought them back to this moment?

"What on earth is going through that fertile mind of yours now?"

She shook her head and brushed her forehead with a nervous hand. "I've lost all perspective. For a weird moment, I wondered if you . . . if you could somehow be responsible . . . for Shawn Delaney's death."

He stared at her. "You think I'm some kind of monster risen from the dead to do the killing all over again?"

Her pulse was rapid as she met his black glare. "You've hated your great-grandfather with an all-consuming passion. As far as you're concerned, Shawn Delaney is responsible for the horrible man your grandfather became and for the inherited weakness that destroyed your father. Men have sought revenge for less cause than that."

His blue eyes hardened. "You're ready to put the bloody knife in my hands, aren't you?"

Her mouth was suddenly parched. "What was the date that Shawn Delaney was murdered?"

He shrugged. "I don't remember the date exactly. Sometime late June, 1888." He cursed himself for not knowing how much time was left before Shawn's death.

She swallowed. "This is the last week in June, 1888."

Colin was silent for a long weighted moment. An ominous tick of a clock sounded in his ears. Finally, he said gruffly, "Then I guess we don't have long to wait before I find out the truth about what really happened . . . and who took their revenge."

"Colin—"

"For heaven's sake," he said wearily. "Quit building a scenario in your mind that doesn't follow the facts. What is going to happen is going to happen. History has already been written."

"Maybe not all of it." Hot tears sprang into her eyes. She knew she was putting aside all logic but she couldn't escape a whirlwind of apprehension just thinking about Colin coming into contact with Shawn Delaney. She didn't want Colin to see her fearful tears so she turned away quickly and walked briskly out of the parlor.

"Della . . . wait."

She ignored him and walked quickly down the hall. A moment later, she heard the front door slam. She brushed tears from her eyes and made her way to Vinetta's room.

Lolly was in the back hall just outside the bedroom door, carrying an armful of linens.

"Good morning, Lolly. You're up and about early this morning."

"Yes'um. Miss Vinnie always changed her own bed," Lolly said, her eyes large and apprehensive as she handed Della a pair of clean sheets and a pillowcase.

"Thank you." Della took the bleached linens that smelled of strong soap.

The girl hesitated as if she wanted to explain. "Miss Vinnie didn't like people in her room."

Della nodded. *Yes, I know.*

Lolly glanced down the hall at the kitchen doorway. "I do your bed if you want. You no tell Miss Inga."

Della was touched by the housemaid's offer. "Thanks, Lolly, but I don't mind changing the sheets. I'm used to making my own bed. Besides, you have enough to do."

"Yes'um." She gave Della a fleeting smile and disappeared into the bathroom with fresh clean towels.

Della went into the bedroom and shut the door. As always, she tensed, waiting for the cloying scent of Vinetta's lilac perfume to invade the room, but a stale musty smell was the only thing that touched her senses. Either the woman's lingering spirit had only been an aberration of her imagination or Vinetta had given up and departed like a well-behaved ghost, Della decided with relief.

She put the linens on a chair, turned to the unmade bed and stripped off the bedding down to a mattress covered in black-and-white-striped ticking. She fanned the clean sheet over the bed and lifted the bottom of the mattress to tuck it under—and that's when her hands touched something flat and hard. She drew out the object.

"What on earth...?" She stared at the book in her hand, a business ledger just like the one Maude kept. Why would Vinetta hide an accounting book under her mattress? Della started to open it, but before she could, the hooked rug moved out from under her feet with a jerk. A cloud of lilac perfume assaulted her nostrils like chloroform.

Della threw out her arms and tried to catch herself as she fell backward. She cried out as her head struck the front of the bowlegged dresser. Her vision blurred and she choked on the suffocating sweet smell of lilac.

She heard someone groaning as she fought her way through layers of swirling gray mist. She put both hands on the side of her head, and realized the sound was coming from herself. Spirals of pain radiated from a bump on the back of her head and her skull felt as if it were going to split in half. Nausea churned her stomach and the floor moved in waves under her.

Wavering, she sat up. She couldn't remember what had happened until the rumpled rug and unmade bed came into focus. She drew in deep breaths of air. No lingering lilac scent. "Damn you, Vinetta."

She waited. Nothing happened.

"I found your ledger!" Della taunted. "That was a stupid hiding place! No wonder you always insisted on making your own bed."

Della knew she was babbling but she couldn't control the words spilling out of her mouth. "What are you hiding, Vinetta? I'm going to find out. You can't scare me. You're dead . . . dead . . . *dead*."

She closed her eyes and leaned back against the dresser, waiting for the pain to recede. Slowly, strength flowed back into her limbs. Her mind began to come out of its cotton batting. Now she knew why the room was haunted by Vinetta's lingering spirit.

Gingerly, she got to her feet. Where was the ledger? She'd been holding it when she fell. Della looked around on the floor but couldn't see it. It was here somewhere. She doubted that even vindictive ghosts like Vinetta could physically spirit things away. Carefully, she went down on one knee and looked under the bed.

"There it is," she said triumphantly as if she and the unseen apparition were playing some kind of game. She sat down on the edge of the unmade bed, opened the book and began searching the pages for Vinetta's secret.

"I'll be damned." The entries were easy to decipher because the bookkeeping system was the same as the one Vinetta had set up for Maude's books.

"I don't believe it," Della breathed in utter amazement. There was no doubt about it. No wonder Vinetta hadn't wanted the ledger to come to light. The bookkeeper had been running her own little prostitution ring right out of Maude's house.

Della examined every page and the moonlighting setup was clear. No more than four girls. The last accounting was for Rose, Alma, Eldora and Dorothy. Della recognized two of the names from yesterday's pay envelopes. Somehow, Vinetta must have set up tricks for them outside the house. She took the same percentage as Maude, one-half of what each girl made. Except for a ten percent cost listed as commission, Vinetta's profit appeared to be free and clear. No overhead of a house to run or the cost of entertainment. She came out better on her four girls than Maude did with her fourteen.

Della thoughtfully closed the ledger and put it back under the mattress. "How did you get away with it, Vinetta?" *Or did you?* Maude had never said how her bookkeeper died. Della's skin raised in goose bumps. "Oh, my God," she breathed as ugly new possibilities formed in her mind.

Chapter 12

Della was at her desk when Maude sailed into the office at about ten o'clock. Her eyes were fiery, like cannons loaded for battle. When she saw all the work done and correspondence laid out on her desk for her signature, she gave Della a sharp look as if there had to be some mistake.

"Good morning," Della said sweetly, enjoying a deep sense of satisfaction that she'd been able to perform her job well enough to deflect Maude's ready tirade. "I think you'll find everything in order."

"Hmmph," was all Maude said as she sat down. She didn't mention Della's absence the previous afternoon but just started issuing orders. "As soon as we finish up last night's receipts, I want you to check all of today's deliveries. Make sure everything gets to the kitchen. Especially the liquor. I want every bottle and keg accounted for." Her nostrils flared and her large mouth tightened. "If the deliveries and the orders don't match, I want to know about it. Understand?"

Della understood more than the woman realized. No telling how much of Maude's liquor Jack had stashed away in the cellar. He probably helped himself every time an order came in. Della blanched just thinking about confronting the horrible man. He'd probably throw a fit, positive that she had alerted Maude about his hidden cache. The man was dangerous. Even now, she trembled remembering the ugly scene in the scullery. He'd left bruises on her arms from the rough handling. Thank heavens she hadn't told Colin about the incident, and her long-sleeved blouse had hidden the marks of the brute's harsh fingers.

"What you daydreaming about?" Maude demanded.

Della stiffened. "Can't someone else check the deliveries?"

Maude's hawk eyes stabbed her. "Is there some reason why you can't?"

"No...I guess not," Della said, backing down fast. She didn't want Maude to know what had happened between her and Jack.

"Then don't be wasting time!"

As Della filled the boarders' pay envelopes, she mentally checked off the names of the women listed in Vinetta's ledger. Rose, Alma, Eldora and Dorothy. Only two of them were Maude's boarders now...Rose and Eldora. She checked some back entries in the ledgers. Alma and Dorothy had been boarders a few months previous but had quit. When Vinetta died? Della wondered. How long had the trusted bookkeeper been making money on Maude's girls? And right under the madam's sharp nose and rapier eyes.

Della lifted her gaze from the pay envelopes. "What did you say Vinetta died of?"

"I didn't," Maude said in a tone that put an end to the conversation.

Della sniffed the air. Was there a faint scent of lilac or was it her imagination?

"I sent Colin for a load of supplies this morning," Maude told her. "When he gets back, check everything out before it leaves the wagon."

Thank heavens, thought Della, relieved. She wouldn't have to face Jack, after all.

Maude handed her a list. "Don't get any ideas. I know you two are thicker than fleas on a dog. Keep your noses clean. Nobody fools Queenie for long."

How wrong you are, lady. Her longtime book-keeper had been running a money-making scam right under Maude's nose, and no telling how long Jack Gilly had been siphoning off liquor and other stuff. Maude Mullen wasn't nearly as sharp as she claimed to be, but Della wasn't about to point that out. She murmured an obedient, "Yes, ma'am."

Maude looked at her pointedly. "Lilyanne tells me you stopped by her room."

"Yes. She seems very nice and I think she's terribly lonely." Della hesitated. "And concerned about the baby."

"Hmmph," Maude grunted.

Della wanted to say something about Lilyanne's determination to keep the child but decided she might only make matters worse by disclosing this information. After all, she really didn't know the whole situation, she told herself. Maybe Lilyanne planned to leave Maude without repaying her for the months she had been given free room and board. "Has she been with you very long?"

Maude ignored the question. "I don't think it's a good idea for you to fraternize with the girls. Better to keep both sides of the house separate."

"Didn't Vinetta make friends with any of your boarders?" Della asked innocently. She watched Maude's expression for some sign that she might have hit a target with the question. Nothing. Not even a flicker of an eyelid.

"Vinnie kept to herself. Spent her free time in her room, knitting or crocheting."

And working on her books, Della added silently. Nothing in Maude's manner indicated that she knew about Vinetta's secret arrangement with two of her current girls. Maybe I'm wrong in assuming that Vinetta was putting something over on Maude, thought Della. There might be another reason for her hiding the ledger under the mattress.

A wagon rumbled down the alley past the office windows and Maude gave a jerk of her head. "The fellows are back."

Della took the inventory list and left the office. She came out in the hall just as she saw Lilyanne's young friend about to hurry up the stairs. The girl was out of breath and carrying another package.

"Good morning, Jenny," Della said, glad that she had remembered her name.

"I...I hope it's all right," the shy girl stammered as she hesitated on the first step. She wore the same drab navy dress and wide-brimmed hat as she'd worn yesterday. "Lilyanne said I could come every morning to see her . . . if I wanted to."

"Of course it's all right," Della assured her.

With a bob of her head, Jenny darted up the stairs as if she expected some giant hand to reach out and grab her.

Maude came out of the office. "Who was that? Who were you talking to?"

"A young friend of Lilyanne's," Della answered before thinking. When she saw Maude's scowl, she wished she'd kept silent. "I think it's good for Lilyanne to have company. It can't be very pleasant sitting up in that room alone day after day."

Maude centered her glare on Della. "Get on with your job. What goes on upstairs is none of your business."

Della bit back a sharp retort. What good would it do to argue, she thought as she hurried into the backyard.

Billy was at the reins and Colin sat beside him in the high wooden seat. The wagon bed was filled with boxes, kegs and baskets of produce.

Colin gave her a wave of his hand as she came out the back door. He was off the wagon in an instant and walked briskly across the barren ground to meet her. He'd been cursing himself all morning for the way he had stomped off after their flare-up. He'd handled the situation all wrong. She was as stubborn as he was and he never knew from one moment to the next what was going on in that active mind of hers. He wanted to keep her safe, and every day that passed, a growing apprehension warned him that it might already be too late.

"Everything okay?" he asked, aware of the golden sheen of her hair as the sunlight touched it. His finger itched to lift the soft wisp of hair curling on her cheek. Her gray-green eyes were deep enough to drown a man. "I'm sorry about this morning," he said quickly.

"Me, too."

She smiled and they stood looking at each other until Billy went by them carrying a sack of flour and gave them a withering glare.

"Wait a minute, Billy," Della said. "I have to check all this stuff in."

"Who says so?"

"Your mother. She seems to think some of the deliveries are getting lost between the wagon and the house. What do you think?"

Billy's freckled complexion turned a blustery red and he looked ready to throw the sack of flour in her face. "You accusing me of something?"

"Cool it, Billy," Colin ordered. "Della's just doing her job. If you've got a beef, take it up with your mother." He took Della's arm. "Come on, I'll help you with the inventory."

The iron gray horse stood listless in his traces while Della and Colin went through every item in the wagon and checked it against the order from the Larimer Street Grocery: chicken, steaks and roasts, pork chops, flour, sugar, eggs, cheeses, fresh fruits and vegetables. Colin had picked up thirty dollars' worth of beer, wine, whiskey and champagne from Aurora Liquors.

They had just finished the inventory, when Jack Gilly came down the steep stairs leading up to quarters above the barn. "What in the hell do you two think you're doing?'' he bellowed as he stomped over to the wagon, his face set in a pugnacious scowl.

"Checking in the delivery," Colin said, his eyes flashing as hotly as Jack's.

"Well, get on with ye," he said with a wave of his thick hand. "Me and Billy will take care of the stuff the way we always do."

"Maybe you'd better make a few changes," Colin warned. "Maude seems to think some of the things are getting lost . . . between the wagon and the house. You know anything about that?"

Jack shot a venomous look at Della. "Somebody better keep their damned mouth shut . . . if they know what's good for them."

"Are you threatening Miss Arnell?" Colin took a step forward. "You'd better think twice about it. Unless you want what few brains you have splattered all over your ugly face."

"Why, you—" Jack jammed his hand into his pocket.

Della screamed when she saw the sharp blade flash in the sunlight.

Colin grabbed Jack's wrist and shoved him back against the wagon. The men twisted and turned. Stumbled and shoved. The knife blade rose and fell, glistening in the sun as they fought for it.

Della cried, "No, no! Stop! Stop!" *It wasn't supposed to happen this way. Not Colin. Not Colin.*

The men crashed to the ground. Blood started coming from somewhere. The crimson flow mixed with dirt on their sweaty faces. Colin raised a foot and slammed it into Jack's groin. With a loud cry, Jack reeled backward, still holding the knife in his hand.

Colin plowed into him and gave Jack's arm a fierce twist. The knife flew up in the air and landed almost at Della's feet.

With a cry of relief, she picked up the weapon. The vision faded of it stuck in Colin's back. She backed up, holding it behind her.

Jack stopped fighting when Colin had him pinned to the ground and demanded, "Had enough?"

"Get off me, you son of a—"

Colin jerked Jack to his feet and Della saw that the flow of blood was coming from Jack's bulbous nose. Thank God, she breathed, weak with relief. Neither of them had been stabbed.

Jack grabbed his bleeding nose and staggered to the pump that hung over a horse trough. He gave the handle several fierce pumps and then cupped his hands under the flow. He threw the water on his face and red rivulets poured down his black beard.

Colin walked over to Della, dusting off his clothes, tucking in his shirt and smoothing back his ruffled hair.

"Are you all right?" she asked.

"Fine." He grinned like a little boy who'd taken on the school bully and won. A gleam of excitement sparkled in his eyes as he wiped blood off his face with his sleeve.

"You enjoyed that," she said, appalled.

"Let's say I dealt with the matter to my satisfaction."

"Well, you look awful."

"You should see the other guy," he quipped and his smile broadened. "I've been wanting to flatten Gilly's nose from the first moment I looked at his ugly face.''

''He won't forget this, you know.''

''Probably not. But I doubt he'll be eager for more of the same. Why did he threaten you about keeping your mouth shut?''

''I don't know,'' she lied.

''Your eyes always turn gray when you're angry...or lying,'' he said. She stiffened when he held out his hand. ''Give me the knife.''

She backed up. ''I'll keep it.''

''Don't you trust me with it?'' His smile was gone.

''Of course I trust you, but...but...'' Her voice trailed off. Shawn Delaney was coming to the house that afternoon. How could she put the knife that might have killed him into Colin's hands?

Chapter 13

"Give it to me. Let me have the knife."

"No," she said, but before she could react, he reached around her back and took it from her.

"Don't keep it," she pleaded. "Give it back."

He glanced over at Jack who had left the water pump and was stomping up the narrow outside staircase to the quarters above the barn. "And why would I want to do that?"

"Because..." She faltered. "Because it would be safer."

He raised an eyebrow. "Safer to have the knife in Gilly's pocket than mine?"

"If that's the knife that killed Shawn Delaney..." Her voice trailed off.

For a moment, he didn't get the implication. Then he gave a curt laugh. "I see. It's me you don't trust with a knife." He waited for her to deny it. When she didn't, he said evenly, "I wasn't around when someone planted a knife in my great-grandfather's back, remember? I can't change what happened—"

"Not *what* happened," she agreed sharply, "but maybe the *way* it happened."

"Do you honestly believe that?"

"I don't know what to believe, but I'm afraid. Let me keep the knife, please."

He set his chin. "There's no reason to assume that this is the knife that murdered my great-grandfather."

"There's no reason to believe it isn't." She searched his face as if trying to find some kind of reassurance. "What's going to happen when you meet Shawn Delaney this afternoon?"

"I don't know," he said honestly. He'd gone over in his mind a thousand times exactly what he would say and do when he came face-to-face with the man he held responsible for his family's sordid genealogy. His hand unconsciously tightened on the knife's handle.

At that moment, Billy came out of the house. As usual, his face was set in a belligerent scowl. He glanced at the inventory sheet in Della's hands. "You got all the stuff written down?"

At her nod, he gave her a hate-filled glare. They could hear him swearing as he began to unharness the gray horse. Della started walking toward the house.

"Will you be around this afternoon?" Colin asked as he reached out and took Della's hand. He wanted to draw her close but he could feel a barrier going up between them.

She pulled her hand away. "I'll be here. I wouldn't miss it. After all, meeting Shawn Delaney is the real reason you rushed into that blasted tunnel, isn't it?"

She waited for him to answer and when he didn't, she said curtly, "That's what I thought."

She went into the house without looking back.

"What's going on?" Inga asked as Della came into the kitchen. "Billy said you're checking all the deliveries."

"Maude's orders. She must be suspicious that some of the supplies are getting lost between the wagon and the kitchen."

"Don't tell me she's finally caught on to that bum Gilly. She's got a blind spot as big as an elephant's foot where that guy's concerned. Everybody would be a hundred times better off if she gave him his walking papers."

"Has he ever been in trouble...for knifing somebody?" Della asked.

"Not that I know about. But I wouldn't put it past him. I always thought he hotfooted it here from Chicago because somebody was on his tail. He's a mean one." Inga gave her a stern look. "You'd do well to give him a wide berth."

"Did Vinetta ever have trouble with him...or Maude?"

Inga wiped her hands on her apron. For some reason, the woman seemed willing to gossip. "Nope. Miss Vinnie always kept pretty much to herself. Wasn't one to cross anyone. Heard she was pretty wild when she was younger but I never saw anything out of the way."

"Did she seem to have...extra money?"

"Extra money?" Inga looked at Della in surprise. "Land sake, the poor woman sent every extra cent she had back to that family of hers. Never talked much about them but I gathered she had a sick mother who needed lots of care. I wondered if her old lady knew whcrc the money came from. She might have rather died than live on earnings from a whorehouse.''

If Inga was aware of Vinnie's little moonlighting business, she wasn't letting on, Della thought. *I wonder if anyone knew about Vinetta's extra income?* Maude had laughed when Della had asked her about her bookkeeper having any money.

Della talked Inga out of a decent lunch, ate at her desk and was still there at three o'clock. Shawn Delaney could come through the door at any moment and every time she heard a noise in the hall, she looked up, her stomach twisting nervously.

Maude had made a point of telling Della that she had no intention of sitting in her office waiting for the councilman to arrive. ''I'll be in my apartment. That double-dealing politician can damn well cool his heels while someone sends word that he's here. And if I'm not in the mood to waste my time, I may not come down at all.''

Della wondered where Colin was. If he was in one of the front parlors, he would know when his great-grandfather arrived. Was he planning a confrontation between them? She worried that if Colin lashed out with all his pent-up anger and bitterness, the meeting could be explosive.

As the moments passed, she couldn't stand the suspense any longer. She pushed back her chair, left the office and hurried down the hall. She gave a quick glance into all the parlors as she passed. In the front hall, an early customer deposited his hat and cane at the door before quietly climbing the stairs to a prearranged assignation.

Where was Colin? Maybe he had decided the time wasn't right for a meeting with his great-grandfather. She shivered, thinking of the way he had taken the knife from her hands. Maybe he was outside on the porch—waiting to intercept Shawn.

She started toward the front door just as a breathless little man with gold-rimmed glasses came hurrying in. He glanced around nervously as if he'd never before been inside a house of ill repute. He stayed his distance from Della, twirling his hat.

"Pardon me, miss. Could you tell me where I could find Mrs. Mullen?" He seemed ready to dart back out the door if Della took a step toward him.

"She's upstairs . . . in her rooms."

The little man took a step backward. "Oh, dear." He glanced at the staircase as if it led to the nether regions of hell.

"I'm her bookkeeper . . . can I be of help?"

"Oh, yes," he said, clearly relieved. Beads of perspiration glistened on his balding forehead. "I have a message from Mr. Delaney. He's unable to keep his appointment this afternoon. An unexpected political meeting. He's very sorry."

Della tried not to let the relief show on her face. "I see. I'll give Mrs. Mullen the message."

"He . . . he said he might be able to make it tomorrow. He'll let her know." He gave a quick bob of his head and fled out the door as if the devil himself was about to grab his coattails.

A smile hovered on Della's lips but it quickly faded when Colin came in the front door, his expression tense. "Who was that?"

"A messenger. From Shawn Delaney. You can relax. He's not coming. Your great-grandfather was delayed by a political meeting." She didn't add that he might come the next day. "Were you waiting outside for him?" *With the knife in your pocket?*

As dark shadows crossed his eyes, she reached out and touched his arm. Whatever the truth about Shawn Delaney's life and death, she feared that the knowledge wouldn't lay to rest the demons that had plagued Colin. Her heart ached for him and she longed to protect him from himself but she felt helpless in the situation. "I wish you wouldn't torture yourself so. What good would it do for you to unleash all the built-up hatred you have for him?" she demanded with a dry mouth. "Why blame all the ugliness of the Delaney men on him. Your grandfather and father were responsible for their own decisions...the same way your mother was. You can't make Shawn Delaney responsible for what you do now."

"I want to meet him face-to-face." His voice was suddenly ragged. He reached into his pocket and drew out the knife and handed it to her. "Maybe I shouldn't tempt the fates. Who knows what'll happen when I meet the bastard eye-to-eye. He's been in my nightmares as long as I can remember...the bogeyman my mother held over me."

Della let out a breath of relief as she gingerly took the knife. "I'll put it safely away. Wait here a minute. I'll be right back."

She hurried to her room and quickly stored the knife under the mattress with Vinetta's ledger. For the time being, the hiding place was as good as any. When she returned to the front of the house, Colin was waiting for her on the porch. She slipped her arm through his. The lines in his face eased as he covered her hand. "Thank you."

"For what?"

"For coming into my life."

"Life or lives?" she teased. "Come on, let's go someplace quiet where we can talk. I've got something interesting to tell you."

He raised an eyebrow. "What have you been up to now?"

"I can't tell you here . . . someone might hear."

He thought for a moment and then led her around the front of the house and down the alley.

"Where are we going?"

He gave her a reassuring wink as he stopped at Trudie's back fence, reached over and unlatched the gate. "Come on."

"I don't think we should. Trudie doesn't like people using her yard, remember?" Della protested. "She'll just chase us out again."

"She's napping. And while the cat's away . . ." He closed the gate and pulled her into his arms. "The mice will play." He kissed her long enough and thoroughly enough to make his point.

Then he took her hand and led her up the steps of a tall latticed gazebo at the left side of the house. A bright pink honeysuckle vine trailed its way to the top of the white structure and blended its fragrance with a sheltered bed of lilies of the valley. Grass redolent of a recent cutting sparkled green-gold in the late-afternoon sun.

They sat down on a circular bench in the gazebo's dappled shade. A quiet loveliness filled Della like the strains of enchanting music. Colin's dark hair, his piercing blue eyes and inviting lips swept her outside herself. She surrendered to his arms and her mouth found his with surging desire. His hands slipped over her back, molding her body to his.

They were both breathing heavily when he eased his mouth away from hers. The heat radiating between them snapped like static electricity. He eased her down onto the floor and, gently parting her clothes, made love to her as if the leaf-covered bower were a separate world.

The depths of her feelings both amazed and frightened her. She gasped at the unbelievable pleasure of his strong body pressed upon hers. Once again, the union between them was both demanding and giving, rising like a crescendo to a peak of mutual fulfillment.

A bird trilled happily in a nearby tree and a murmuring breeze sent the green leaves quivering. When he finally slipped away from her, she opened her eyes and looked up into his face with a warm glow of satisfaction. His knowing smile softened all the hard lines and planes of his mouth and cheeks and made his eyes as clear as a cloudless heaven. "Are you happy?" he asked, tracing her lips with his finger.

"Wonderfully."

"So am I. For the first time in my life. I never knew what making love was like before now. And to think I had to go back over a hundred years to experience it."

He kissed her again, but with his words the halcyon mood had been broken. Reluctantly, they righted themselves. Colin chuckled as Della tried to get her tousled hair back into a prim twist. Somehow, a pearl button on her blouse had been popped off. If Maude saw her—

"Oh, my gosh," Della said with a start. "I forgot to tell Maude that Mr. Delaney wasn't coming. She'll be furious with me."

"She's figured it out herself by now," he said gruffly.

"I suppose so."

"What was it you were going to tell me? Something important?"

"I don't know how important it is . . . but curious. I found a ledger hidden under Vinetta's mattress. A detailed record of income from four girls...two of them are Maude's current boarders, two of them worked here but quit. I checked Maude's books this morning and there's no record of the tricks that Vinetta recorded in her ledger."

He raised an eyebrow and whistled softly. "So Maude's trusted bookkeeper had a little something going on the side."

"Not a *little* something. These girls brought in good money, as much as thirty dollars for an all-night stand. Vinetta split their earnings fifty-fifty and the only expense she recorded was a ten percent commission she paid to somebody...probably a guy who arranged the tricks."

"And Maude never found out?"

"I don't know." Della shivered. "I wondered if...if maybe Vinetta's death wasn't all that natural. If Maude did find out, she would have been capable of exacting revenge."

Colin tightened his arm around her shoulders. "I wouldn't put anything past that woman. That's why we have to be careful. If she gets suspicious about us, no telling what she'll do."

A cold ripple chased up Della's back.

"Better forget about Vinetta. Don't make any waves asking about her death."

"The woman's spirit is still around. I know that." She touched the back of her head. "When I found the ledger, the rug flew out from under me. I fell and hit my head. See." She ducked her hand and gingerly pointed to the spot.

"I don't believe this. Are you telling me you think that some ghost made you fall?"

"I don't think it—I *know* it. Vinetta hasn't wanted me in her room from the beginning. The first morning, she almost suffocated me." She buried her head against his shoulder. "I know I'm not imagining it. I just know it!"

He put his lips against her cheek. "You're the most intelligent, capable and brave woman I've ever known." He lifted her chin and looked deep into her eyes. "If you've had these experiences with some lingering spirit, I believe you."

Della let out a shaky breath. "Thank you. At first, I thought Vinetta just didn't want me in her room, using her things, but when I found the hidden ledger, I wondered if that's what she didn't want me to find."

"But if she's dead, what difference would it make?" Colin asked.

Della thought a moment, then said, "Maybe Vinetta wants to protect someone...someone who was in the scam with her."

Colin thought a moment. "Someone who got the ten percent cut?"

"Could be." She put her head in the cleft of his shoulders and closed her eyes. "I don't know. And I don't really care. Vinetta's shady dealings are safe with me. Maybe her spirit will be satisfied to move on if I destroy the ledger."

Colin rested his head against hers. Then he moved his lips to the soft crevice of her earlobe and lightly teased her with a flicker of his tongue. His arms tightened around her. Dear God, how was he going to keep her safe? There were threatening forces on all sides. When he came face-to-face with Shawn Delaney, he didn't know if he could control his need for revenge, his need for relief from the demons that had plagued him all his life. His mother's voice would forever damn him for being a coward if he walked away from a confrontation with his great-grandfather. He groaned and pressed his face against Della's. She represented everything in his life that had been missing. This giving and sharing was completely foreign to him. And now that he'd found her, he feared that fate would take her from him.

Della returned to her room, buoyant and deeply contented. A glow remained from the tender moments she had spent with Colin. Everything was going to be all right. He cared for her, and she was falling in love with him. She had never felt so complete, so optimistic that they were strong enough to meet all the challenges that might face them.

When she opened the door and went into the bedroom, her smile faded and her sense of well-being shattered instantly. Vinette's room had been ransacked. Immediately, Della ran her fingers under the mattress. The knife and ledger were gone.

Chapter 14

"*What should I do?*" Della viewed the tumbled drawers, emptied wardrobe and stripped bed. Clearly, someone had been searching for something. The knife? The ledger? Or something else she didn't know about? Della took a deep breath. No hint of perfume. Vinetta's lingering spirit had gone. If Vinetta had been trying to protect someone, as Della suspected, the dead woman had failed.

Della began to put everything back in the precise order that Vinetta had left them. Nothing would be accomplished by drawing attention to the ransacked room. She was fearful of setting in motion dangerous events that might make her presence in the house more precarious than it was already. Her hands were trembling when she finished and a growing apprehension replaced the confidence that being with Colin had given her.

* * *

Della spent a restless night, worried about Shawn Delaney's promised visit and the knife that was in some unknown person's hands. At least Colin didn't have it, she reassured herself, and then the old fear stabbed her that somehow he would turn out to be the culprit.

Finally, the pearly light of dawn edged the drawn curtains. Another day. Another twenty-four hours caught between two dimensions of time. Wearily, Della looked through Vinetta's wardrobe for something halfway comfortable to put on. She finally decided on a mauve silk dress that Vinetta might have worn as second best. A prim inset of lace decorated the bodice and several rows of matching edging circled two layers of skirt.

After she'd put it on, Della was surprised how flattering the mauve was to her blond hair. She never would have chosen the color. Impulsively, she added an amethyst brooch from Vinetta's black lacquered jewelry box. As she pinned the brooch on her high collar, Della waited for some protest from the dead woman but the room remained clear of lilac perfume. Vinetta's spirit seemed to have departed after it had failed to prevent the secret ledger from being discovered.

And what about Inga? Had she known about Vinetta's profitable scam? Della was positive the cook knew more than she was willing to admit.

Nobody was in the kitchen when Della passed by on her way to the office. As always, the house was quiet in the early-morning hours. She wondered how Colin's evening had gone and felt a deep stab of loneliness as she began to record last night's receipts.

When she heard kitchen sounds, she left her desk and came out of the office door just as Lolly came down the hall with a breakfast tray.

"Oh, thank you," Della said, reaching to take it from the girl.

"No, miss." Lolly shook her dark head. "Not yours. I take the tray up to Miss Lilyanne."

"Oh, I'm sorry. I thought...wait a minute. I'll do it," Della said impulsively.

Lolly looked anxious. "Miss Inga might not like."

Della gave her a reassuring smile. "It's all right. Just put my tray on my desk. I'll be back down in a couple of minutes."

Della took the tray from the girl and carefully mounted the stairs. It was a little after six o'clock. Maude wouldn't be down until ten or eleven and a visit with Lilyanne might take the edge off the unpleasant start to the day.

She went down the darkened hall to Lilyanne's room. The door was open and as she peeked in, she was surprised to see the pregnant young woman wearing a pale pink bonnet with a wide ribbon tied under her chin and a lacy white shawl draped over her bulging figure. She was putting on her gloves, obviously getting ready to go out.

"I brought up your breakfast tray," said Della.

"Oh, how sweet of you, Della. Just put it over there. I'm on my way to confession. I'll eat when I get back...after communion."

Della placed the tray on a small table beside the rocking chair. "It'll be cold."

"I know." She gave a light laugh. "I'm used to it." She picked up a rosary and slipped it inside a beaded purse. "Are you Catholic?" she asked with a hopeful edge to her voice.

Della shook her head. "My Aunt Frances was Lutheran and I guess I'm not much of anything."

"Oh, too bad." Lilyanne sighed. "It would be nice if we could walk to Saint Elizabeth's together. I hate being out on the streets alone even for a few blocks. People stare, you know. Easy to tell what they're thinking—a woman in my condition shouldn't be out in public."

Della opened her mouth and then closed it. The old stigma that kept pregnant women out of sight was firmly entrenched in Lilyanne's day. No use expressing women's rights to Lilyanne who would have no frame of reference for understanding them.

"The church is only a few blocks from here. A nice walk, really. And I hurry back before very many people are out. Maude warned me about making a spectacle of myself. It would be nice if I didn't have to go alone but—"

"I'll go with you," Della said. "And if anyone stares at you, we'll stare right back."

"Would you, really?" Her sky blue eyes were luminous. "Just think, I was feeling lonely when I woke up this morning. And a little frightened, too. And look what happened? My guardian angel sent you to change all that."

Della didn't want to argue that her role as guardian angel was as far from the truth as anything could be, so she just smiled. "I like taking early-morning walks, myself."

While Lilyanne waited in the front hall, Della returned to her room and put on the straw hat and picked up Vinetta's purse. Her stomach was growling with emptiness and as she passed through the kitchen, she grabbed a couple of hot muffins that were turned out on a cutting board to cool. She heard Inga growl but she just gave a wave of her hand as she ate them on the way out of the kitchen.

She didn't meet anyone in the hall and she took Lilyanne's arm as they left the house. Colin must still be at the boardinghouse enjoying Trudie's ample breakfast table, she thought as they walked past the house. She looked up at the windows of his room. The memory of their passionate lovemaking brought a flush of warmth surging through her, and a deep-seated longing that was a demanding ache.

Something in her expression must have made Lilyanne ask, "Are you in love, Della? I don't mean to pry, but is there someone inside that house whom you care about?"

Della nodded.

"And he cares about you?"

"Yes, I think so."

"Then you must hold on to him."

"I'm trying," Della said wryly.

"I didn't try hard enough," she said with a quiver of her lips. "I gave up too easily."

Della waited for Lilyanne to go on but the young woman put an end to the subject with a vague frown that discouraged any comments from Della.

As they walked down the street, Della realized again how heavy with child Lilyanne was. Della felt her heart constrict. She couldn't bear to think of Lilyanne going back to working Maude's trade. Was that the only option she had? Della glanced at Lilyanne's angelic face and decided that there had to be something better for her. But what? An unwed mother with a sordid past had only one way to go—down.

"Father Sanisteven is kind enough to let me take private communion after confession." Lilyanne gave Della her sweet smile. "He's going to help me keep my baby."

"Why doesn't he do something to get you out from under Maude's roof now?" Della demanded. "Don't throw your life away, Lilyanne." *Stop what you're doing before it's too late.* A mocking inner voice reminded Della that she had said the same thing to her sister but Brenda had stubbornly clung to a life-style that had killed her.

Lilyanne's lips quivered. "It doesn't matter what happens to me if . . . if I can keep my baby."

Della bit back a flood of protests. She was filled with anger and frustration knowing that nothing she could do would change anything. *You can't live somebody else's life.* Lilyanne's fate and that of her unborn child had already been set.

"Della, if something . . ." Her voice wavered. "If something should happen to me . . . will you make sure that my baby is put into Father Sanisteven's hands?"

"Don't talk like that." Della couldn't promise Lilyanne anything. She didn't know from one minute to the next when fate would send her back to the twentieth century.

"Promise?" Lilyanne insisted.

"I will if I can," Della said honestly.

Saint Elizabeth Catholic Church stood on a narrow lot that was barren of trees and showed every evidence of a struggling parish. The interior of the church was dimly lit by sunlight slanting through colored-glass windows and candles flickering on both sides of a modest altar. Lilyanne went directly to a small room at the left side of the sanctuary while Della waited in one of the back pews.

Several poorly dressed women came and went, leaving behind lighted candles that smelled strongly of melted lard. Della's thoughts were in limbo and the peace that seemed to come to other worshipers evaded her. When Lilyanne appeared a few minutes later, a tall round-shouldered priest with gray hair walked with them to the front door.

"This is my friend, Miss Della Arnell," Lilyanne said to Father Sanisteven.

When the priest fastened his slightly veiled eyes on her, Della couldn't break the steel-like lock of his penetrating gaze. *Was it possible he saw a different aura around her? Could he tell that she was from a different lifetime?* She felt her deepest secret stripped bare before him. The conviction that he could read her thoughts was so strong that she was stunned when he said with ordinary politeness, "Pleased to meet you, Miss Arnell." He touched the cross hanging on the front of his habit. "You will be a blessing to Lilyanne in her time of need."

"I . . . I hope so," Della stammered.

He gave her a knowing smile before he turned away and disappeared into the dark cavern of the church.

"Isn't he impressive?" Lilyanne said enthusiastically.

"Very," answered Della, wondering what on earth had made her react to the priest in such a stupid way. She had read all sorts of things into his expression and manner. What would the poor man have done if she had started blubbering about being transported a hundred years back in time?

They strolled away from the church and had gone a couple of blocks, when suddenly Lilyanne stopped in the middle of the sidewalk. With a groan, she touched her bulging stomach and a grimace crossed her face.

"What is it?" asked Della, alarmed.

"I...I don't know," Lilyanne gasped, trying to get her breath. "A pain...all the way around my middle." She stood frozen in a hunched position for a long minute. Then she slowly straightened up. "There, it's gone now." She gave Della a faint smile. "I guess the baby is moving around a bit."

Or ready to be born, Della worried silently. "Stay here, I'll get a hired hack to take us back to the house."

"Oh, no. I can walk. It's not far."

"We'll hire a cab. I'll pay for it." Thank heavens, thought Della, she hadn't eaten up the whole five dollars she'd found in Vinetta's purse. They were only three blocks from Maude's house but the distance was too great if Lilyanne was going into labor. "Just stay here. I'll go to the corner and find a hack."

Would a hansom cab stop for a single woman waving frantically so early in the morning? Several went by without looking in her direction before she was finally successful in flagging one down.

The driver was a husky fellow who looked stronger than his swaybacked old mare. Unshaven, his spiky black eyebrows matted in disapproval when he saw Lilyanne. Della was afraid he might refuse to take them.

"Maude Mullen's Pleasure House," Della ordered with a toss of her head.

He muttered something obscene into his straggly beard and Della had to hold her tongue as she helped Lilyanne into the cab.

"I could have walked," whispered Lilyanne, her eyes round with apprehension. "I don't know what came over me."

I do, Della said silently. *You're going to have a baby.* How much did Lilyanne know about childbirth? Surely she knew something about the ordeal ahead of her.

"Are you sure you can afford this?" Lilyanne said worriedly.

"I'm sure," said Della with a stubborn set of her chin. The tired old horse clopped down the street at a sluggish pace that put Della's nerves on edge. The nag wanted to stop every few feet and Della was afraid it would fall dead in its traces any second.

"The poor thing," murmured Lilyanne.

Della kept watching her, waiting for a sign of another contraction. They had almost reached the house when Lilyanne's expression changed and she clutched her protruding middle. "Ohhh," she groaned.

About ten minutes apart, Della calculated.

"Oh, my," gasped Lilyanne when the contraction eased. Her pretty blue eyes rounded in fear. "Do you think that—"

"I don't know. We'll have to call a doctor."

Lilyanne shook her head. "No doctor. Maude said she'd arrange for a midwife when my time came."

The hack jerked to a stop in front of the house. Della hurriedly put some coins into the driver's dirty hand and helped Lilyanne into the house.

"Oh, there you are," said Jenny who was coming down the stairs. "I was just up to your room." Lilyanne's young friend held up a tied package. "I thought you might be needing a few of your things—"

"We have to get Lilyanne upstairs," Della broke in. "Get her to bed."

Jenny's brown eyes widened with sudden fright.

"It's all right, Jenny," Lilyanne quickly assured her. "It's just that . . . the baby's getting restless."

Della and Jenny helped her mount the stairs. She had another contraction before they reached her room. Neither Lilyanne nor Jenny seemed to recognize early labor. Hadn't anyone told them what happened in childbirth? Lilyanne's eyes widened in fright as she clutched her stomach.

"The uterus is contracting," Della explained, but clearly the medical explanation was lost on both of them.

Jenny's young face was as perplexed as Lilyanne's. "What'll we do?"

"Get her undressed and into bed. I'll alert Maude. Don't panic. This could take hours. You're going to need your strength, Lilyanne. Try to eat some breakfast." Della bent down and kissed the young woman's moist forehead. "It's going to be all right. Don't worry."

"Bless you, Della." Lilyanne squeezed her hand. "Thank you for... for being my friend."

Della turned away before Lilyanne could see her eyes misting. She hurried down to the second floor to Maude's apartment. It was too early for the woman to be up. Maude would be furious at being disturbed but dammit, this was an emergency.

Della knocked briskly on the door but no one answered her frantic knock. "Maude," she called. Her voice echoed through the somnolent halls. She tried the doorknob. Unlocked. Della poked her head through the half-open door. "Maude?"

No answer. Della pushed the door fully open and went in. It took a moment for her eyes to adjust to the dark sitting room. Dark blobs of furniture crowded the center and lined the walls. The room was like an antique store crammed with chairs, sofas, glass cabinets. Every surface was covered with figurines, lamps, glassware, china and indefinable bric-a-brac.

"It's Della," she said and waited. "Maude?" Her only answer was a nasal snore that floated through the open door of an adjoining room.

Della hesitated, almost losing her courage. Waking up Maude could be as disastrous as poking a dozing cougar. Only the desperate need to get Lilyanne help made Della willing to approach the sleeping madam. Gingerly making her way around the islands of furniture, she prayed that she wouldn't knock something over before she reached the bedroom.

She knocked on the open bedroom door but the humped figure in the canopy bed didn't move. The rhythmic snoring never changed; like a foghorn, it rose and fell with each breath. The bedroom was even darker than the sitting room. A dusty, closed smell made Della wonder if the curtains and windows were ever opened. A heavy, sickening odor of smoke turned her stomach. *Did opium smoke smell like that?*

Della pulled back heavy red drapes at the windows and secured them with a thick gold cord, revealing lacy curtains beneath. The sun came through the curtains and made dappled shadows on a floral rug. The bedroom was as crowded with furniture as the sitting room. A woman as broad as Maude must have to turn sideways to move around, thought Della as she eyed the narrow passages.

Screwing up her courage, she walked over to the bed. "Maude, wake up!" She put a firm hand on Maude's soft shoulder and shook her.

The woman broke off in midsnore, gasping and choking. With her mouth hanging wide open, she opened her glassy eyes and for a moment she looked like a grotesque witch not dead, but not alive. The woman's head was nearly bald. Her neck skin hung loose, and large blotches of ugly brown spots were dabbed with some kind of bleaching cream.

Della quickly removed her hand. "Maude, I'm sorry to wake you but—" She never finished.

The woman screeched, rose abruptly and gave Della a shove that sent her reeling backward. Della went nearly to her knees before catching herself.

"Get out! Get out!" Maude's filthy tongue filled the room with abusive swearing. Della had never heard such language. She knew that Maude would never forgive her for this embarrassment. The woman's pride had been shattered. Della had seen the woman at her worst. Bald. Ugly. Without adornment. And there was nothing Della could do or say to remedy the situation.

"Didn't you hear me?" Maude screeched.

"I think everyone on this floor can hear you," Della said evenly. "I apologize for the intrusion but we have an emergency."

"An emergency? A goddamn raid!" In an instant, she had her emotions under control. "Those bastards. They know the house is quiet this time of morning." She grabbed an elaborate red wig sitting on a crowded night table and plopped it on her head. She reached for a lace-edged handkerchief and began cleaning her face.

"It's not a raid, Maude."

She stopped wiping her face. "Then what in the hell is it?"

"It's Lilyanne. I think she's going into labor."

Chapter 15

"What in the hell are you blabbing about?"

"Lilyanne is having contractions. Labor." Good grief! Did everyone hide their heads in the sand about having babies? "She may be getting ready to deliver."

Maude's nose narrowed. "This is the emergency that made you break into my bedroom?" Her eyes glinted like polished steel.

"I didn't break in...the door was unlocked." Della stood her ground. "And I think Lilyanne's welfare is important. She needs medical attention."

Maude snorted. "Medical attention. These gals drop babies like pinecones off a tree. If Lilyanne's looking for someone to hold her hand, she's in the wrong house."

The woman's cold indifference dismayed Della. She could have been talking about a stray cat instead of a human being. Lilyanne deserved better. "Do you know if Lilyanne has any family?"

"Never asked. Ain't none of my business. When a gal walks in the door, she leaves her other life behind. That's the way I like it."

"Do you have any idea who the father is?"

"Hell, no. She was already tumbled when she showed up at my door."

Della blinked. "What? You mean she was pregnant when she came here? Lilyanne isn't one of your girls?"

"She is now." Maude set her big mouth in a hard line. "I've been carrying her till she can earn her keep. Some fellows really go for that sweet innocent look, you know. It's about time she began to pay me back."

Della's temper flared. "I guess you'll have to wait a few more hours to recover your investment. She said you were going to arrange for a midwife. I think you'd better call her."

"Oh, you do, do you?" Maude stabbed a stubby finger at her. "Let's get something straight, Miss High-and-Mighty. I do the thinking around here. Got it? You keep your nose in my books and out of my business. And don't ever show your face in my apartment again."

"What about the midwife?" Della persisted.

Maude looked ready to throw something at her. She growled, "Tell Billy to go after Consuelo Chavez. Now get the hell out of here! I'll deal with you later."

Della's stomach was churning as she fled the apartment. Colin was in the front hall when she came down the stairs. He took one look at her ashen face and his chest tightened. He had awakened that morning with a heavy sense of time running out. "What's happened?"

She caught her lower lip. "I may have gotten myself fired."

He put his arm around her trembling shoulders. "Let's go back to the office and talk."

"I've got to find Billy and send him for Consuelo Chavez."

"Who's she?"

"A midwife. It's Lilyanne." Della told him about going to church with Lilyanne and what had happened on the way home. "She's having contractions about ten minutes apart. I...I went to Maude's rooms and...and woke her up. She was furious."

Colin couldn't help smiling when Della described the way Maude had looked without wig, paint and jewelry. "Not at her best in the morning, I gather?"

"A witch all the way around. That woman has a cash box for a heart. Doesn't care what was happening to Lilyanne. Just wants her on the job as quickly as possible."

Colin saw Della's eyes turn an angry gray. "It's not your life," he warned her. He knew she was ready to fight this young woman's battles even if it jeopardized her own situation. "Lilyanne has made her own choices...just like your sister made hers. You're not responsible for either of them."

"Maude's taking advantage of her. Lilyanne was pregnant when she came here and that mercenary woman saw the chance to turn her into a boarder. Lilyanne deserves better."

"How do you know?" Colin asked quietly.

"Because...because I really like her," she said lamely. "And I'm going to help her all I can. Now, I've got to go find Billy."

"I'll give him the message. You stay away from him and Jack. I don't trust either of them." He saw her face lose its color. "What's the matter? Have they been bothering you?"

"No," she said quickly, "but I almost forgot to tell you. Someone ransacked my room yesterday while we were in Trudie's garden." Her anxious eyes locked with his. "The knife's gone."

Damn. He should have kept the blasted thing when he had it. "Don't worry about it." He feigned unconcern. "It'll turn up." The minute the words were out, he wished them back.

Della turned a sickly color. "Whoever took the knife stole Vinetta's ledger, too."

"I don't see how her little scam can involve us," he said, but he wasn't sure. Hell, he wasn't sure about anything. He pulled Della close and felt her slender body melt into his. Maybe they should leave the house this minute. Even as the thought flickered across his mind, he knew that the forces that had brought them back to this time and place were stronger than any will of his own.

Colin found Billy sitting on a keg in the barn, chewing a thick wad of tobacco and whittling at a stick. The glowering kid let go with a stream of brown juice when he saw Colin. His thick mouth spread in an ugly yellow grin when the tobacco spit barely missed Colin's coat sleeve.

"Good thing you're a bad shot." Colin stood over Billy, his hands itching to grab him by the scruff of the neck and knock him off his perch. "Otherwise, I'd have to cram that tobacco wad down your throat."

Billy scooted sideways off the barrel. He hunched his shoulders and thrust his broad head forward. Colin waited for Billy to make a move toward his pocket. If he had the knife, he might be reckless enough to show it, thought Colin. He waited, but the boy just stood there, glaring at him.

"I have a message from Maude," Colin said. "She wants you to go for Consuelo Chavez."

Billy's scowl deepened in his freckled face but he didn't raise his fists or reach for a weapon.

Colin jerked his head toward the barn door. "Now. Get a move on."

Billy hesitated. Then he spat something under his breath and trudged out of the barn and across the yard. Colin watched him until the boy disappeared down the alley.

Maude kept Della busy in the office all morning. She barked orders, piled the work high and warned Della that she'd better keep her nose in the books if she didn't want it cut off. Maude's complexion was sallow, her eyes heavy-lidded and she moved in slow ponderous steps. Her mouth was held in a perpetual hard line. When she snapped something about Shawn Delaney never showing up the afternoon before, Della kept quiet. She wasn't about to tell her that Delaney had sent a messenger with his regrets.

"The conniving bastard knows better than to show his face around here. If he tries to get his hands on my house, he'll live to regret it," Maude said with a toss of her piled-high wig.

Or die trying, Della silently corrected with a churning in her middle. Would Colin's great-grandfather come back today? She prayed he wouldn't.

Maude got up from her desk at about eleven o'clock. "I'm going to the dressmaker's." She glared down her twitching nose at Della. "And I want you here when I get back. Don't be running off like you've been doing. I know what's going on. I've had enough of your dillydallying. You and that Colin fellow sparking around under my nose. Keep your mind on your job, understand?"

Della held her tongue. She knew that Maude would have already booted her out the door if she hadn't needed her to handle the books.

After Maude left, Della tried to concentrate on entering figures into the ledgers but she couldn't keep her thoughts away from Lilyanne. What was happening? Were the contractions false labor? Had the midwife come? She wanted to run upstairs and make certain someone was with Lilyanne.

About one o'clock, as she was debating whether or not she dared go upstairs, she saw Jenny go by the office door heading in the direction of the kitchen. Della ran into the hall and caught up with her. "Jenny, wait a minute."

The young girl turned around. She looked tired and worried. Della searched her drawn face. "What's happening? How's Lilyanne?"

Her lips trembled. "She's having a hard time of it. Six hours and no sign of the baby. I'm worried."

"Is the midwife with her?"

"She says we can't do anything...but wait. She says the baby will come when it's ready but Lilyanne is wearing out." Tears flowed into the corner of Jenny's eyes. Della wondered how many births the teenager had seen, if any. "I don't know how long this can go on...the baby not moving."

"Lilyanne's stronger than you think," Della said with as much optimism as she could muster. She knew that some women were in labor for an unbelievably long time... *but they had the help of modern medical science to get them through.*

"What if she dies...here...in this awful place?" Jenny cried.

"Stop thinking like that."

"I can't help it. I don't know what to do," she wailed. "I don't want to break my word...but—" She broke off.

"What do you mean, 'break your word'?"

Della saw the shutters go down on Jenny's thin face. "Nothing. I don't know anything. I...I have to get some water." She fled into the kitchen, leaving Della staring after her.

The girl's words puzzled Della. She and Lilyanne must have been friends before Lilyanne came to Maude's house. And if the madam was to be believed, Lilyanne was already pregnant when she came to the bordello. Jenny must know something that was causing her distress.

Della walked thoughtfully past the office and up the stairs to the third floor. Lilyanne's door was closed and a small Mexican woman with gray hair answered Della's knock. She only opened the door a crack and

Della couldn't see in. "What you want?" she asked in a heavy Spanish accent.

"Lilyanne? How's she doing?"

"We wait," the woman said briskly.

"Is there anything I can do?"

"Say prayers to Mother Mary." Consuelo shut the door.

Della turned and walked slowly down the hall. She met Jenny on the third-floor landing carrying a large kettle of water. Even in the dark corridor, Della could see her red-rimmed eyes.

"I want to help, Jenny. If you know something that will help Lilyanne, please tell me."

Jenny shook her brown head, fled past Della and disappeared into Lilyanne's room.

Maude came back to the office at two o'clock. She eyed the work Della had done, then handed her a pile of invoices to record. She didn't ask about Lilyanne, and Della didn't volunteer any information.

A few minutes later, Jack Gilly strode into the office. "I need to talk to you, Maudie... private like. You ain't going to believe what's been going on under your nose." He sent Della a withering glare and plopped Vinetta's red ledger down on Maude's desk. "You'll never guess what I found."

"What is it?"

"I ain't sure."

"Where'd you get it?"

Jack's moist mouth curved in a smirk. He pointed his hairy finger at Della. "Under a mattress in her room. I was looking for my knife and this was hidden in the same place."

"This belong to you?" Maude held up the ledger.

Della shook her head emphatically. "No, I discovered it yesterday when I was changing the linens. It must be Vinetta's." Della tried to keep her voice neutral. "I'm not sure what it is."

Maude opened the ledger. Her hawk eyes quickly stabbed the pages, her mouth growing tighter and tighter.

"Is it important?" Della asked with feigned innocence.

"Don't be stupid," Jack snapped at Della. "If that belongs to Vinetta, she was up to something. Hell, there's dollars and cents all over them pages. She was fleecing you, wasn't she, Maudie? Skinning the goose right under your nose?" His tone bordered on the gleeful.

Watching Maude's complexion deepen to an ugly purple, Della was pretty certain that Maude had never seen the material before. She turned the pages, examined each entry and let go with a flood of swearwords. "That low-down conniving cheating bitch!"

"I was right, wasn't I, Maudie?" Jack taunted with a smirk.

Maude slammed the book shut and leaned back in her chair as if she'd been delivered a mortal blow.

"I never did like that self-righteous Vinnie. She didn't have me fooled none," Jack proclaimed, sticking his hand in his vest in a pompous way. "I could have warned you. Hell, that woman would have bilked her own mother if she had the chance . . . and after all you did for her, too, Maudie. Taking her in when you knew she was a jailbird just out of the coop. Some people have no sense of loyalty."

Maude's head slowly came up from her chest. Her eyes narrowed as if her thoughts were spinning like a slot machine. Her eyes suddenly rounded. She turned to Jack. "Get out!" she ordered in a low guttural groan. "Get out, you bastard."

Jack's mouth dropped open and his hand came out of his vest pocket as he straightened up. "What the hell? Why you swearing at me? I brought you the damn book, didn't I?"

"A good way to cover your tracks. Get out of my sight before I tear that lying tongue of yours right out of your mouth."

Jack shot Della a venomous glare as if Maude's anger was all her fault. "Women!" he muttered as he stomped out of the office.

Maude motioned to Della. "Come here." She flipped open the ledger and put her pudgy finger on one of the columns.

Della looked at the figures. "That's an account payable. A debit. Ten percent of the gross earnings."

Maude thoughtfully pursed her lips. "Vinnie paid someone ten percent of what she took in?"

"That's what it looks like."

Maude clenched her hands and stared down at the columns of figures. "She had someone arranging the tricks. Someone right under my nose."

"Could it have been Jack?" Della asked.

Maude put her head in her hands. "He'd do anything for money. Never gets out from under his gambling debts." She slowly raised her head. "Vinnie could have used him as a pimp."

"But he didn't have to bring you the ledger," Della said, puzzled.

"A smart move. He figured you'd tell me about it, so he decided to get here first and float the skunk stink in a different direction."

Somehow, Della didn't think Jack Gilly was sharp enough to be a manipulator. When she said so, Maude jerked around, her eyes blazing. "Then who in the hell could it be?"

"Maybe one of your customers."

Maude's glare darkened. "Vinetta was sure as hell working hand in glove with someone. Using my girls on the sly, she was. I still can't believe it."

"How did Vinetta die?" Della watched Maude closely. "Did she have an accident?"

"Naw. She got sick. Some disease that turned her eyes and skin yellow."

Probably hepatitis, thought Della. Thank heavens. It was a relief to know that the woman had died of natural causes.

"And a good thing she's dead," Maude said as if echoing Della's thoughts. "I'd strangle her with my bare hands if I could."

Della shivered. Just thinking about the explosive showdown between the two women was enough to make her thankful that Vinetta had escaped Maude's wrath. But if Vinetta had not died as a result of foul play, why was her spirit still hanging around? The whispered answer came from out of nowhere, leaving Della more certain than ever.

To protect someone.

Chapter 16

Maude's face was blotchy with anger. "Go upstairs and tell Rose and Eldora to get their butts down here. Don't tell them what it's about."

"I don't remember which room—"

"Second floor. Eldora's the first one on the left and Rose is across the hall. Tell them I'm waiting. If they aren't down in five minutes, I'll drag them down by their hair in their nightclothes. We'll see who's running this place."

"What about the other two women... Alma and Dorothy?"

"They left the day of Vinnie's funeral. Never could understand why. The lying cheats were afraid I might find out about their double-dealing. I'd like to have about five minutes with them now," she growled.

Della quivered just thinking about being in Rose and Eldora's shoes. She knew Maude wasn't making an idle threat. She would exact payment for their treachery in some form that would satisfy her hurt pride and her bank account. Della wondered whether she should warn the girls and give them a chance to slip out of the house.

Don't get involved, Colin had warned her when she told him about Lilyanne. *You can't change anything.* She knew he was right but it didn't make the task any easier. She dreaded rousing the two women from their beds and sending them down to the vicious madam.

Eldora swore as she opened her door to Della's insistent knocking. Her dull eyes rimmed with dark shadows hinted at a lack of sleep. "Dammit!" she swore when she saw Della standing there. "What the hell do you want?"

Della recognized Eldora as the dark-haired woman who had been sneaking back into the house just before dawn. No doubt she'd been returning from her moonlighting job. "Maude wants to see you in her office within five minutes. And...and she looks ready to peel the skin from your bones," Della added to emphasize the urgency of her message.

"Why? What's the matter?"

Della turned around without answering, knocked on Rose's door and delivered the same message to the blond woman. A weary, dissipated Rose exchanged frightened glances with Eldora, who was still standing in her doorway. "Do you think that Maude ...?" stammered Rose, her plump figure trembling.

"Shut up," Eldora snapped.

"But what if—"

"Let me do the talking, for God's sake, Rose." Eldora slammed her door.

Rose just stood there, her large frightened eyes like those of a child who knows she's going to get a beating. For a moment, Della was afraid the terrified young woman would throw herself at her, weeping and pleading.

"Don't keep her waiting," Della said and hurriedly left Rose standing in her doorway. Della doubted very much that she could remain detached if Rose started asking her questions. Lifting the skirt of her mauve dress, Della ran lightly up to the third floor to check on Lilyanne.

Consuelo opened the door a crack. "Baby not come yet."

Della could hear Lilyanne moaning and crying inside the room. "Can I do anything?"

"We wait." The door shut.

Della wanted to pound on it and demand to be let in. But what good would that do? It might release some of her own worry and built-up tension, but her intrusion would do Lilyanne little good. She stayed out in the hall, pacing, praying that the baby would come soon. Her affection for Lilyanne made the vigil a torturous wait. Finally, she gave up and went back downstairs.

Maude's office door was shut and she could tell from the raised voices that Rose and Eldora were in the office with the madam. Shouting, weeping and wailing rose and fell in loud crescendos. Time to make herself scarce, Della decided. She didn't want any part of the ugly scene.

Della headed for the kitchen and Inga stopped kneading a blob of bread dough when she entered. The cook jerked her blond head toward the din of shouting and crying. "What in saint's name...? Sounds like a bunch of cats having a snarling fur fight."

A good description, thought Della. "Beats me," she said.

"What do you mean, 'beats me'?"

"Just an expression." *Too modern for you.* Della picked up an apple and bit into it.

Inga's eyes narrowed. "Jack's running around like a bear with a can tied to his tail. Never seen him so ready to crack somebody's head open. I pity anyone who gets crosswise with him."

The bite of apple grew in Della's mouth. What if Shawn Delaney showed up at the house while tempers were at combustion level? If Colin was right about his great-grandfather's being killed the last week of this month, the murder could happen anytime.

"I think I'll lie down for a while," she told Inga.

"You quitting work this early in the day?" Inga scoffed. "It's only three o'clock."

At that moment, they heard Maude bellowing down the hall. "Della! Della! Get your behind in here!"

Inga gave a satisfied grunt as she filled a pan with rolled biscuits. "I guess Maudie ain't through with you yet."

Della's steps were slow and reluctant as she made her way back to the office. She expected to see Maude stomping around the room, throwing things, ranting and raving. Instead, the madam was sitting at her desk, slumped heavily against the back of her chair, her double chins almost resting on her ample chest. Rose and Eldora were not in the room.

The silence was like ice that would shatter with the slightest quiver of air. Afraid to speak, Della stood in front of Maude's desk, waiting. What had happened to crush this formidable woman? Had she learned that her ever-loving Jack Gilly had truly betrayed her? He seemed to be the only one she really cared about. Anybody else she would have sent packing long ago. Maude exploited everyone, but not Jack Gilly.

Della waited a long minute and then asked quietly, "Did you find out what you wanted to know?"

She nodded.

So Rose and Eldora had talked. It was apparent from Maude's devastated visage that she must have found out firsthand all about Vinetta's exploitation. "I can't believe it," she said in a choked voice.

She must have learned the identity of the ten-percent accomplice. Della couldn't stand the suspense any longer. "Was it Gilly?"

Maude raised her head. Her eyes were glazed with pain. She shook her head. "Not Jack. But I would have understood if he'd been the one. I learned long ago not to trust him. He's not got an honest bone in his miserable body. And he's stupid. All hot air. He'd never be able to carry off something like that under my nose." The dejected lines around her mouth deepened. "No, it wasn't Jack."

"Then who?"

She rested her head in her broad hand for a moment and then raised it. "Trudie."

"Trudie," Della repeated, unable to digest the name for a moment. "The landlady? Gertrude Katz? But she . . . she told me that she was glad she'd gotten out of the business." The statement must have been a bold-faced lie. Apparently, the woman had kept her finger in the prostitution game, after all. Her boardinghouse was only a clever front. Colin had said it was filled with working men. Why walk across the alley, when a man could get pleasured in his own room? Had Colin known about it? If he had, why hadn't he said something? Maybe he guessed it was Trudie when she'd told him about Vinetta's ledger. She felt a swell of anger. What else had he kept from her?

Maude looked bilious. "My oldest and only friend. What a fool I've been."

"What are you going to do?"

"I haven't decided."

Maude's cold words were like the rattle of a snake. Della shivered, remembering what the malicious woman had vowed. *No one crosses Maude Mullen and gets away with it.*

Della braced herself for the order that would pull her deeper and deeper into the ugly mess. "What do you want me to do?"

"Don't tell anybody about this! Understand? Nobody."

Della nodded in relief. "But what about Rose and Eldora?"

"I'll keep them on until I decide how to get even with Trudie." Her nostrils flared. "They'll pay me for every trick they turned for Vinnie and Trudie if they have to sell every stitch of clothing they own." She rose to her feet. "I'm going up to my room and I'll skin the person who bothers me with anything!" She landed heavily on the last word as she flung the threat over her broad shoulder.

A minute later, Colin poked his nose into the office. He whispered, "I just met the battle-ax in the hall. What on earth has put her on the warpath?" He came over and perched on the edge of Della's desk. "What gives, sweetheart?"

He was taken aback when she glared at him, her eyes snapping with anger. "Why didn't you tell me Trudie was offering more than just room and board to her houseful of men?"

"What are you talking about?"

"You know damn well what I'm talking about."

He held out his hands in a gesture of bewilderment. "You'll have to give me a hint."

"Gladly. Remember the ten percent Vinnie was paying out? Well, the two girls involved told Maude that it was your friendly landlady who arranged the tricks. It seems that Vinetta ran the business, the girls provided the services and Trudie took her cut for providing the customers."

He let out a slow whistle. "Are you sure?"

"Of course I'm sure. What I want to know is why you didn't say something—"

"Because I didn't know. I've never seen any sign of hookers in the boardinghouse." He frowned. "I've been in and out of the place all hours of the day and night. If there had been girls in the house, I would have seen something. Besides, the fellows would have been talking." He shook his head. "No, I don't believe it."

"But...but, it has to be true," she argued. "Rose and Eldora said so. They told Maude that Trudie was involved."

"Della, I don't know what story they're telling, but you have to believe me. Trudie is not using any of Maude's girls or anybody else to keep her boarders happy. I'd bet my life on it! Hey, don't look so shaken. Come on, let's get out of here before there's ten more things for me to do." He looked at his pocket watch. "It's almost four o'clock."

He drew her to her feet and kissed her slowly and tenderly. A surrendering tremble flickered through her body. Gently cradling her face in his hands, he deepened the kiss.

He was always stunned by the power she had to shut down every facet of him except total feeling. She took him away from all he had ever been. Making love to her was addictive, but he reluctantly drew away.

"Want to take a walk with me? I have to run one more errand for Maude. There's a flower stand in the next block and she wants me to pick up some fresh flowers for tonight. Come with me and I might even sneak a rosebud for my lady."

"Is that a bribe?"

He kissed the tip of her nose. "The best one I can think of at the moment."

She laughed softly and some of the tension of the day eased away.

They left the office and started down the hall just as the front door opened and Shawn Delaney walked in.

Chapter 17

Della shot a look at Colin and saw his eyes narrow in a flash of black hatred. His hands clenched and every muscle in his body seemed to contract in a hard spasm. She instinctively stepped in front of him in a feeble attempt to become a barrier between him and his great-grandfather.

"Good afternoon." Shawn doffed his derby hat and gave her his politician's smile. He wore a fashionable long jacket in dark green, cut away to show a matching waistcoat, matching trousers and a white shirt with a starched collar five inches high. His dark hair fell around his broad face with the same casual thickness as Colin's and his dark eyebrows had the same arched flare over dark blue eyes. Once again, his build and general likeness to Colin sent an enveloping weakness surging through her.

"G-good afternoon," she stammered, still trying to block Colin and keep him behind her.

"So we meet again...Miss Arnell," Shawn said pleasantly. His glance went over her shoulder, lightly touched on Colin and then swung back to Della as if he had little interest in the man standing behind her.

She was astounded. Couldn't he see the family resemblance between himself and Colin?

"Will you tell me where I can find Maude Mullen?" he inquired.

"I'm afraid she can't see you this afternoon," Della said with a rush, wanting to get Shawn out of the house as quickly as possible. "She's...indisposed."

Colin brushed past Della. "Maybe I can help you. Mr. Delaney, isn't it? I've waited...years...to meet you face-to-face." He positioned himself in front of Shawn, his shoulders stiff and his blue eyes as hard as obsidian.

Shawn looked surprised and a little taken aback by the aggressive tone. "And you are...?"

"Nobody you'd give a damn about. But I know several people who have had to live with the results of your miserable greed and ambition."

Shawn's eyes were suddenly as cold as Colin's. "I don't know who you are, sir, but I take objection to your tone and insinuations."

"Take all the objection you want, *sir.* Before I'm through—"

Della grabbed his arm. "Colin, please. This won't do anybody any good. Let it go...let it go."

Before Colin could respond, there was a light step on the staircase behind them and then a gasp of surprise. "Oh, no!" At the girl's choked cry, Shawn

looked past Colin and Della to the staircase. "Jenny?"
An expression of utter amazement crossed his face.

The young girl put her hand on her mouth, and
turned to flee back up the stairs, but Shawn's commanding voice stopped her. "Jenny! Come here. I
don't believe my eyes. What in the world are you doing here? Explain yourself."

Jenny came down the stairs with slumped shoulders and tearful eyes. She began sobbing. "I didn't
know what to do, sir. I wanted to come to you, but
Lilyanne made me promise—"

"Lilyanne? What has she got to do with this? She's
in Europe. You were her personal maid. You must
know that her parents sent her away."

She shook her head. "No. They lied to you . . . to
everybody."

Shawn's face went stiff and he was clearly having
trouble shaping words with his rigid mouth. "But
she . . . what . . . what are you saying?"

"Lilyanne's parents didn't send her away."

"But I don't understand."

Jenny's mouth quivered. "Lilyanne ran away . . . and
she's been hiding here . . . till the baby came."

Shawn's face was suddenly as white as bleached
bone. "Baby?"

"Yes, sir . . . she's . . . she's . . ."

He grabbed the sobbing girl by the shoulders. "Why
didn't you come to me? You knew how things were
between us. How could you keep this from me?"

"She made me promise . . . didn't want to ruin your
life . . ."

His voice broke. "It was ruined the day she disappeared from my life. Where is she? I'll get her out of here."

Tears streamed down Jenny's face as she sobbed hysterically. "Lilyanne...she...she's in a bad way. The baby came but...I'm afraid..."

"Take me to her." Shawn pulled Jenny up the stairs as he took them two at a time, and the next instant they had disappeared in the landing above.

Della was too stunned to move. Colin walked to the bottom step and looked after them. Then he sat down on a step and put his head in his hands.

"Shawn...and Lilyanne," Della said in an incredulous tone as she eased down beside him. Her thoughts were going in every direction like dry leaves whipped in a devil's wind. *Shawn Delaney the father of Lilyanne's baby?* Sweet, lovely Lilyanne so much in love that she was prepared to disappear from her lover's life by hiding out in a bordello? She wanted to protect his reputation and his future even if it meant sacrificing her own life.

Della went over everything Lilyanne had told her. Everything seemed to verify that she was trying to protect her lover. And what about Shawn Delaney? After meeting Edith, his cold, self-righteous wife, Della could understand how he could fall in love with someone as happy and vivacious as Lilyanne. Suddenly, her heart ached for both of them.

"An adulterer, on top of everything else," muttered Colin.

She touched his sleeve. "Maybe you shouldn't be so hard on him."

"Are you defending him?"

"I'm trying to understand him. And that's what you should do. I think Shawn loves Lilyanne deeply and I know she loves him. Obviously, he was unhappy in his marriage and they were caught in a no-win situation when they fell in love. And when she knew she was pregnant, she ran away to protect his reputation. Apparently, the family lied to him and told him that Lilyanne had gone abroad. Only her maid, Jenny, knew where she was and Lilyanne must have sworn the girl to secrecy. Lilyanne was going to have his baby without ever telling him." Tears caught in her throat. "I can't condemn either one of them."

Colin rose to his feet. "I don't agree with your assessment of the situation. Shawn Delaney is a selfish bastard who never cared for anyone but himself."

"How do you know?" she countered. "Your mother poisoned your mind against him and because you resembled him, she put a guilt trip on you. You owe it to him to find out the truth—isn't that why you've been waiting to confront him?"

"All right. I'll get the truth from his own lying lips." He took the stairs two at a time the way Shawn had done.

Lilyanne's door was open and Jenny was out in the hall sobbing. "A doctor's coming," she told Colin in a choked hushed voice. "But . . . I think it's too late. She's almost gone."

Colin slowed his steps and hesitated in the doorway of Lilyanne's room. The stench of blood and death was so strong that it curdled Colin's stomach. Shawn sat on the bed, holding a wan Lilyanne in his arms, and the midwife was in a chair gently rocking the newborn baby.

Tears flowed down Shawn's cheeks. "My beloved...my dearest love...why...why didn't you tell me? I was ready to give up everything. My marriage...my career." He pressed his wet face against her cheek. "You're the only good thing that's ever happened to me. I wanted to be worthy of you. I truly believed I could make the city better and cleaner. But without you, nothing matters. I love you, Lily. Please don't leave me." His voice broke.

Lilyanne's lips curved in a weak smile. "You have a daughter," she said in a whisper. "She matters..."

Colin turned away from the doorway and walked slowly back downstairs. He felt depleted, like someone who had geared himself for battle only to find there was no enemy. Shawn Delaney wasn't the Lucifer he had hated all his life.

Della stepped forward to meet him at the foot of the stairs. She searched his face anxiously, but before he could say anything, all hell broke loose out in the street.

Chapter 18

Della and Colin rushed to the window. She couldn't believe her eyes.

"What in blazes is going on?" swore Colin.

Flag-waving, banner-carrying men and women crowded the street from curb to curb. Drumrolls, brassy horns, shrill whistles and cowbells made a boisterous accompaniment to shouts of "Clean up Market Street." Raucous jeers came from spectators lining the sidewalk and dumbfound customers emerged from saloons, illicit houses and cribs. The parade of shrieking women shook their fists at men and prostitutes. "Down with the devil!" they cried. "Up with righteousness."

Della could almost feel the foundation of the house rock with vibrations from the bombastic parade. Maude suddenly appeared from somewhere, swearing as she pushed between Colin and Della. "What the hell?"

"Some kind of demonstration," Della said with a tight throat. She knew from a banner printed Citizens' Civic League what organization was behind the march. She groaned inwardly and shot an anxious glance at Colin. Did he realize that this was his great-grandmother's club?

At that moment, a small bearded man with a medical bag pushed his way through the crowd and bounded up the front steps. Colin hurried to open the front door.

"Dr. Freedman," the man said briskly.

"Upstairs, third floor, last room on the right," Colin said.

The doctor nodded and walked right by Maude without acknowledging her presence.

"What are you doing here?" she demanded, but Dr. Freedman continued to ignore her and went up the stairs.

"It's Lilyanne," Della said quickly. "She had the baby but...she's..."

"She's dying!" Colin interjected angrily. "Damn you, Maude. Why didn't you see that she had proper care?"

"How dare you?" Maude's face turned an ugly red. "Are you telling me how to run my house?"

"I'm telling you that if that girl dies, you ought to be run out into that street and let the crowd have its way with you."

Her voice pulsated with anger. "We'll see who gets thrown out in the gutter. Jack...Jack!" Maude yelled.

Colin gave her a twisted smile. "He's across the street. Buying drinks for everybody, and laughing behind your back as he does it. You ought to hear the way he talks about you."

Maude choked, her eyes flashed wild with anger. "Get out! Nobody talks to me that way. If I ever lay eyes on you again, I'll...I'll see you tossed in the river with concrete for shoes."

Della grabbed Colin's arm "Let's go." He didn't move. "Please...please, let's get out of here."

"Better listen to her while you have the chance," Maude snarled.

At that tense moment, Jenny came down the stairs, sobbing, her hands pressed against her lips. She raised anguished eyes to Della.

"Is...Lilyanne...?" Della choked on the question.

Jenny nodded and her shoulders shook with new sobs. Della put her arms around the girl and they held each other, tears streaming down their faces. Della couldn't believe that Lilyanne's bright, happy spirit was gone. She'd never met anyone so brave and so giving. A soul like that didn't deserve such an end. Della's pain was washed with anger.

The doctor came down the stairs and slammed his hat on his head. "Too late to do a damned thing."

"I called a midwife," Maude protested.

Dr. Freedman just glared at her without answering as he opened the front door. He had just pushed his way outside into the crowd, when Shawn came downstairs, holding the tiny bundle of his newly born daughter. His sunken eyes, drawn face and numbed shock added years to his face.

"Shawn Delaney!" Maude screeched and positioned her bulky frame in front of him as he reached the bottom step. With hands on her hips, she demanded, "What are you doing in my house?" Her eyes fell to the bundle in his arms. "And where in the hell do you think you're going with that baby?"

"I'm taking her with me," Shawn said in a pain-weary voice.

"You ain't doing nothing of the kind."

"She's mine. I'm her father."

The flat statement took Maude aback for a second and then a gleam of avarice crowded out the surprise in her eyes. "You ain't takin' nothin' out of this house without my permission. She was born here...you want the brat...you pay for her."

"Go to hell." Shawn tightened his hold on the baby and pushed past Maude with a deliberate shove that nearly sent her fat legs out from under her. He opened the door, stepped out on the porch, but was blocked from going down the front steps. Billy had been standing on the porch, watching the surging crowd fill the street and spill onto the sidewalks.

"Stop him, Billy," screamed Maude. "Get that baby."

A knife came out of the boy's pocket. Brand-new and shiny, the one Colin had seen him whittling with earlier in the day. Billy waved it in front of Shawn.

Colin moved quickly out the door just as a woman screamed and pushed her way onto the porch.

"Shawn," cried Edith. "What are you doing here? Dear Lord in heaven, what is going on?"

Colin pushed between Shawn and Billy. "Give me the knife," he ordered, moving forward toward the threatening blade. With a menacing advance, he forced Billy to back away from the front door.

Edith stood on the bottom step, staring at her husband, her eyes pinned with disbelief upon the baby in his arms.

"It's mine...mine and Lilyanne's," said Shawn quickly. "I'm taking her home." He started down the steps.

Billy gave a wild cry and lunged. Colin brought his hand up and clipped the boy's wrist. The knife went sailing out of Billy's grasp and landed at Edith's feet.

She picked it up and followed her husband who was ahead of her, pushing into the crowd. A moment later, a cry went up from the milling crowd as Shawn Delaney fell to the ground with a knife buried in his back.

Chapter 19

Della and Colin pushed through the crowd to Shawn's side. He had twisted when he fell so that the baby was protected in his arms. He weakly held the bundle up to Della. "Don't let...Maude...have her," he gasped. Then he closed his deep blue eyes and drew his last breath.

"Let's get out of here," Colin growled. Della clutched the baby to her chest, and before anyone realized what was happening, Colin maneuvered Della and the baby through the crowd. Just as they reached the other side of the street, utter pandemonium broke loose.

Women screamed.

The marching demonstrators scattered.

Flags and banners were tossed to the ground as the parade became a hysterical mass of running, screaming people. "Killer on the loose."

Colin and Della didn't look back as they fled down a side street and through many trash-filled alleys until they were several blocks away from the slain Shawn Delaney.

They were both breathing heavily when they slowed their steps. Della's lips trembled and tears filled her eyes as she cradled the newborn in her arms. She couldn't believe what had happened. The whole ugly scenario played over and over in her mind and only the warmth of the baby pressed against her chest made the tragedy real.

Colin stared down at the sidewalk as they walked. *His great-grandmother!* How could it be? The ugly heredity that flowed in his veins had come from her...and not from his great-grandfather. Edith must have twisted his grandfather into the mean man that he became. Her bitterness and hatred for the husband who had betrayed her must have been heaped upon her son, Ian. His grandfather must have grown up with his mother's bitterness. *Just the way I grew up with my mother's,* thought Colin.

Della stopped in the middle of the sidewalk and jerked his thoughts back to the moment. "There's only one thing to do," she said. "Lilyanne made me promise to take the baby to Father Sanisteven if something happened to her."

"No, we can't..."

She stared at him. "What do you mean, we can't?"

"We have to take care of her." His voice broke. "She's family."

His stubborn glare turned her skin cold. "She's your great-aunt and belongs to a different time...she lived over a hundred years before you!"

"I know...but...but I can't give her up to strangers."

"Then...then you're not going to try to find your way back...to your own time?" Della's chest was suddenly so tight, it threatened to crack with the next breath.

He didn't answer.

"Don't you want to live your *own* life...in your *own* time?" She could see the struggle going on within him.

He walked another block in silence and then gave a deep ragged sigh.

"What is going to be...is going to be," she reasoned quietly. "You can't change the next hundred years because you don't like what happened to your forefathers."

"I wish to heaven that I could!"

"Isn't it enough that you can shape your own life? Make it anything you want?" she argued. "I believe you were given an insight into the past so you could know what really happened to your great-grandfather—a deep-seated love brought about Shawn Delaney's death."

Colin looked as if he were suddenly blinded for a moment. "What are you saying? My great-grandfather has been haunting me and brought me back into his lifetime because he wanted me to know the truth?"

"Doesn't that make as much sense as anything?"

"Yes," he said thoughtfully.

"You were given a chance to see into the past...but not to change it. If the baby is meant to be put in the priest's care, either we help carry out her fate or it will be accomplished without us."

Colin looked down into the perfect little infant face and the burden on his heart lifted. If the love Lilyanne and Shawn had for each other was fulfilled, the fates would treat their love child kindly.

They found the priest in the small graveyard beside the church as if he'd been waiting for them. He took the baby without any questions.

"What will happen to her?" Colin demanded.

"One of my parishioners, a young mother, lost her baby yesterday. Her heart will be healed with this new blessing. The Lord works in mysterious ways, his wonders to perform," quoted the priest.

"We...we would keep the baby if we could," Colin told him as if compelled to express the pain he felt at giving her up. "But we...we can't stay here."

Father Sanisteven nodded as he fixed his solemn eyes on them. "I understand. Time is like pebbles upon a beach, carried away only to be brought back to shore again." He made the sign of the cross and then disappeared into the church, the baby cradled in his arms.

Della turned and buried her face against Colin's chest. He gently guided her to a patch of soft green grass under the spread of a giant oak tree. They sat on the ground and slowly drew strength from each other and from the serenity of the peaceful churchyard.

"What will we do now?" Della leaned her cheek against his. "We can't go back to Maude's. Do you think she really would have made Shawn pay for his own child?"

Colin's face was grim. "She would do anything for money."

"Do you think she knows we took the baby?"

"I don't know. If she does, she might put the law on us. She has enough policemen on her payroll."

Della shivered. The late-afternoon sun suddenly lacked any warmth. "You mean she might accuse us of kidnapping?"

"Who knows how her mind works. In any case, we better make ourselves scarce."

"But the tunnel! How can we find it if we can't be seen on her property?"

Colin pushed back a shock of dark hair in an impatient gesture. "Maybe we should try to come at the tunnel from the other direction—the hotel?"

"No!" Panic surged up in her throat. "It's too dangerous. Shawn warned me not to go into the hotel, as if he knew that I might be sucked into some existence that could trap me forever. His ghost was the one I saw with the phantom harlots and I thought it was you. I'm afraid. I don't want to chance it. We have to find the other end of the tunnel."

"I've looked ... you've looked. There's no tunnel leading to Maude Mullen's Pleasure House."

She stiffened.

"What is it?"

"Maybe we've been looking at the wrong house." She turned to him with a sudden brightness in her eyes.

His forehead creased with puzzlement and then smoothed. "You're thinking that—"

"That maybe the tunnel didn't go across the street to Maude's but to Trudie's boardinghouse!" she said excitedly.

"I suppose it's possible," he said hesitantly.

"We know that Trudie was collecting ten percent on Vinetta's string of girls. Rose and Eldora fingered her as Vinetta's accomplice. Why would she get ten percent unless she was providing some needed service?"

"Like a passage to the hotel across the street." He let out a slow whistle. "I'll be damned."

"You said you'd swear that no women were turning tricks in the house proper."

He nodded. "Trudie runs a clean house. Her boarders would talk if she didn't."

"That morning I saw Rose and Eldora coming into the house, they just appeared. They could have been slipping across the alley from Trudie's place."

"What are you saying?" Colin asked.

"We've been looking in the wrong place. It wasn't Maude who was using a tunnel to take advantage of trade in the hotel across the street, but Vinetta and Trudie."

He was thoughtful. "If you're right, the location of the passageway has been under our nose all the time. Damn, I never thought to have a look around the boardinghouse. I remember noticing a cellar door when we were sitting in the garden. And I mentioned hearing voices in Trudie's garden. No wonder she didn't want anyone spending time there."

"The tunnel must come out in her basement. The girls exit out the cellar door, go through her garden, out the alley gate and back to Maude's house." Her eyes grew wide. "Now that I think about it, when we were swept through that tunnel and deposited on Maude's doorstep, there was a riot of colors and a heavy scent of perfume. Trudie's garden!"

"We could be wrong," he cautioned.

"But we could be right."

"Don't get your hopes up. All of this is only speculation." He leaned over and kissed her warmly. "But if there's a tunnel in Trudie's house, we'll find it."

Chapter 20

They decided to remain in the churchyard until after dark. As the sun slipped behind the mountains on the western horizon and twilight spread across the valley, they leaned up against the trunk of the oak tree and talked quietly.

"I was wrong," Colin admitted, his voice thick with emotion. "Shawn Delaney wasn't the Satan of my nightmares."

Della was relieved to hear him put his change of heart into words. Now he could lay his hatred to rest. Be free of the obsession that had tortured him for so long.

"At first he may have intended to use the Market Street properties for his own benefit," reasoned Colin, "but falling in love with Lilyanne changed him. He loved her enough to give up his ambitions, his family..." His voice choked.

"And Lilyanne loved him enough to run away and hide in a brothel so he wouldn't have to give up his ambitions and family," she said. "They were willing to sacrifice themselves for each other." Her own eyes were suddenly moist. "I believe that in another time and place, they'll find each other again...and...and live happily ever after."

A shadow of a smile crossed his lips. "You surprise me. I didn't know you were an incurable romantic."

"I didn't know it, either." She brushed her lips across his mouth. "Until you taught me."

When the streetlamps came on, they left the churchyard and walked a block to a hole-in-the-wall café. Della had run from the house without hat, gloves, purse or wrap, but Colin had a handful of change in his pocket, enough for two cups of coffee, some cheese and brown bread. They took a back table and no one in the dimly lit café seemed to notice them. The other poorly dressed customers looked like people who had as little money in their pockets as Colin.

Everyone was talking about the murder of Shawn Delaney. "Right in front of Maude's place."

"Them do-gooders better stay in their end of town, that's all I got to say."

"His poor wife was just a few feet away when it happened. They sent her to the hospital."

"Damn politicians are always stirring things up."

"Poking their noses where they don't belong."

"I heard a woman was bending over him and ran off with something. The cops are looking for her."

Della spilled her coffee over the rim of her cup as she set it down. Her eyes widened with sudden panic.

"Me! They're looking for me. Someone saw me take the baby from Shawn."

Colin reached over and covered her hand. "Just rumors. Don't pay any attention."

"Maybe we should go to the police . . . ?"

"No," he said sharply. "Too risky."

"But what . . . what if someone identifies me?" she whispered anxiously. "Maude would love to put a noose around my neck just to get even. You know how vicious the woman can be. Oh, Colin, I wish we didn't have to go anywhere near her house."

"Maybe you shouldn't. I've been thinking. There's no reason for both of us to go. Why don't you stay here and let me have a look around Trudie's. If I find something, I'll come back for you."

She was coward enough that his suggestion was a great temptation. But she quickly shoved it aside. She remembered the way both of them had been swept inside the mouth of the tunnel. What if that happened again? What if he found the passage and was carried into the opening, disappearing without her? She couldn't chance it. She shook her head. "No."

"Why not?" he protested. "This idea about the tunnel being at Trudie's may turn out to be nothing but faulty speculation on our part. It's going to take time and a lot of luck to check the house and property. Nobody's looking for me—"

"I don't care. You're not going anywhere without me."

"Della, be reasonable."

"Save your breath. If and when we find the tunnel, I want to be there."

"And if we don't find it?"

She gave a lift of her chin. "Then we'll stay here."

His blue eyes deepened and touched her face tenderly. "You're some brave lady."

"Not really. I just know what I want. And now that I've found you, I don't intend to lose you...now or ever."

He started to say something but a well of emotions stopped him. What if there was no tunnel? How would he keep her safe? Where would they go? How would they survive in a time not their own? He shoved aside a nagging apprehension that their travel back a hundred years had been a one-way passage.

"All right. Come on. Let's go," he said with stern abruptness to cover up a sense of impending disaster.

Market Street showed little evidence of the afternoon's debacle. A few trampled posters lay crumpled in the gutters and a few discarded streamers caught on lampposts fluttered weakly in the nighttime breeze.

The saloons were brightly lit and tinny music floated out into the street as rowdy customers pushed their way in and out of the swinging doors. Maude's Pleasure House was obviously offering business as usual. A man being murdered almost on the doorstep had not lessened the flow of men in and out of the house.

"I wonder what she's doing for a bouncer," Colin said as they stood in the shadow of a building across the street.

"Maybe she put her ever-loving Gilly to work."

"I doubt that she could keep him away from the booze long enough."

"I really thought it would be Jack's knife that was used to kill Shawn. But he wasn't even around when it happened and the knife Billy had was new. He must have just bought it." She shivered. *Just in time for the murder.*

Colin's eyes narrowed as they traveled to the boardinghouse. Even as they watched, the lights in all the first-floor windows dimmed. "Trudie's turning in," Colin said. "Must be ten o'clock."

Maybe we ought to wait a few hours, thought Della. There was a lot of activity on the street and their chances of running into someone who might recognize her were great. Where could they go to wait? Every time someone looked at her, she was sure the person would stop, point a finger and say, "She's the woman who was running away." Nervous sweat moistened the palms of her hands. She didn't want to cross the street and expose herself to anyone connected with Maude.

"The back of Trudie's house should be dark," said Colin as if reading her thoughts. "Our best bet is to slip down the alley and let ourselves into the backyard by the side gate. If our reasoning is correct, that outside cellar door will lead us down into the basement...and to the tunnel." He slipped her arm through his. "As soon as the street is clear and there are no pedestrians on the sidewalk, we'll stroll across to the boardinghouse."

He emphasized "stroll" as if he knew she was fighting an overwhelming urge to flee the scene as fast as she could. She took a deep breath. "All right. Let's stroll."

They watched several wagons, carriages and hansom cabs go by in the street, then Colin nodded, tightened the guiding touch on her arm and they started across the street. They had reached the other side when Billy came out of nowhere. He must have been smoking around the side of the house when he saw them walking down the sidewalk.

He threw down his cigarette, turned and raced into the house, letting the screen door bang behind him.

"Damn," swore Colin. He pulled Della into the alley and they raced between the two houses to Trudie's back gate. Colin reached over, unlatched the lock, and they bounded inside, quickly shutting the gate behind them.

Della put a hand over her mouth to stifle her heavy breathing. Moonlight through the branches of leafy trees sent a dappled pattern of light and shadow across the yard. One dim light showed through the back door and sent a muted spill of illumination down the back steps. Their presence flushed a night bird from the top of the gazebo and its piercing cry sounded loudly in the echoing night.

They pressed against the house, waiting for any sign that someone inside had seen them enter the yard. When the only sound they heard was the complaint of the irate bird, Colin took her sweaty hand in his and, hugging the shadows, they made their way to a pair of nearly flat cellar doors built against the house. The wooden doors had handles in the middle so each door could be opened and laid back to allow passage down into the hole. Della was reminded of pictures she'd seen of old-fashioned potato cellars.

Colin pulled back on one of the doors and it opened with a loud screech. The rusty hinges sent a message that was verified by the dirty, unused steps disappearing into the black abyss under the house—nobody had used this cellar entrance for a long time. Certainly not girls dressed in satin and lace on their way to sexual assignations.

Colin's face was in shadow but Della knew what his expression must be. He must be feeling the same sickening disappointment that plummeted her spirits to bottom level.

There was no tunnel in Trudie's cellar.

Colin closed the cellar doors just a moment before there was a soft sound of footsteps outside the alley gate, and they heard the latch opening. Colin grabbed Della's hand and they scurried behind a planting of junipers. Crouching they peered through the needled branches and saw a woman slip through the yard and mount the back steps to Trudie's house. Instead of going in, she knocked briskly.

A moment later, a light came on and Trudie opened the door. "What— Have you lost your mind, Rose? Coming over here this early...and in the middle of the week."

"I had to warn you. Maude knows...about everything," Rose said on a sob. "She's got Vinetta's ledger...and Eldora told her about you." Rose's voice quivered. "I'm running away...tonight. But I couldn't leave without warning you."

Trudie cleared her throat. "You're a good girl, Rose."

"You were always square with me and...I'm sorry to cause you trouble," whimpered Rose.

"Don't worry. I'll take care of Maude. I've got enough dirt on her to keep her in line for a long time. You need some money?"

"No, I've got some put away. I...I think I'll go back to Nebraska. There's someone there who may still have me."

"Good luck. Now scoot before someone knows you're here." Trudie stayed on the back steps watching as Rose turned and fled out the gate. Instead of going back in the house, Trudie came slowly down the steps and walked directly toward the evergreen bushes where Colin and Della were hiding.

She knows. Somehow she knows. Della was prepared to stand up and face the consequences, but Colin held her down. He even put his hand over her mouth to keep her from making a sound.

Trudie's shoes clicked on the brick path as she walked. They could hear the rustle of her dress, and when she passed them, they heard her murmuring under her breath. She followed the path to the gazebo and then disappeared around the back of it. They heard a door open and close and the next minute, Trudie came back into view. She passed the place where they were hiding without slowing her steps, and the next minute they heard the back door close behind her and the inside light went out.

Colin gave a satisfied mutter as he eased Della to her feet. A leaping joy made her want to cry, laugh and shout all at the same time. Now she knew who Vinetta had been trying to protect and why Inga had refused to talk about the tunnel. There was no doubt in Della's mind where they would find the tunnel they had been seeking.

"Want to bet?" she whispered to Colin as they left their hiding place.

"I'll tell you in a minute," he hedged.

As they circled the vine-covered gazebo, she thought how ironic it would be if they had made love directly over the passage they had sought.

A tall narrow door opened easily under Colin's touch. Moonlight illuminated a wide landing, lanterns hanging on a wall and candles and matches in containers on a shelf. A cold draft flowed out of the passage but the vicious suction they had experienced before was gone. There was no mysterious urgency. No indefinable force. Only a quiet waiting silence.

"Apparently, the choice is ours." Colin turned solemnly to Della. "We can gamble that we will find our way back to our own time ... or be caught forever in a twist of time that may never let us go."

For a moment, she hesitated, unsure that she should trust herself to make the right choice. Then she smiled. "Let's go home."

He put his arm around her waist and they descended together into the waiting passage.

Chapter 21

Colin took a lantern from the shelf, used a match to light the wick and then held it out in front of them as they descended the steps into the narrow passage. The dirt floor had been swept clean and the smell of new timbers bracing the walls and roof marked the tunnel as fairly new. The sound of their quickened steps echoed in the underground chamber as they cautiously moved forward.

Della clutched Colin's hand as they walked side by side. The lantern made a radius of light around their feet. Braced for the wild sucking force that had driven them forward the first time, she was surprised when only a faint movement of air touched their faces. A growing uneasiness tightened her shallow breathing. She shot a quick glance at Colin's shadowed face. Was he thinking the same thing? Where was the bizarre, unearthly sensation that had assaulted them before?

What if the time warp could *not* be reversed by going back through the tunnel?

She must have gasped for he tightened the grip on her hand. "Steady."

Maybe their assumption had been terribly wrong. She had been convinced that once they found the tunnel, they would emerge from the hotel opening and be back in their own time. But the tunnel appeared to be exactly what it was—a narrow passage dug under the street. Vinetta's girls had made numerous treks through to the hotel without incident. What if she and Colin reached the exit without anything happening?

"Something doesn't feel right." Her voice quivered with suppressed fright. What if they kept walking and never reached the other side? What if they were somehow lost in the hundred years between the past and the present? Doomed to wander in the purgatory of an endless tunnel? She stopped. "Let's go back." She couldn't see his face clearly but she knew from his tone of voice that he wasn't about to retreat.

"Back to what?"

"I don't know...but I'm afraid."

He slipped a firm arm around her shoulders. "It's going to be all right. I know it," he lied. He didn't know anything of the kind but he did know they couldn't remain stranded between two lifetimes. They had to move in one direction or another. "Come on. Let's get out of this hole."

"Why...why is it so different this time?"

He had been wondering the same thing. The damn tunnel was too ordinary...a dirt passage under the street and nothing more. He wouldn't have been surprised if they had overtaken a couple of Maude's girls walking ahead of them.

"Listen!" he said as a thunderlike rumbling sounded overhead. They could feel vibrations like waves coming through the earth. Something heavy rolled over top of them and loose dirt trickled down the walls.

"Hurry." He urged her forward as the vibrating rumbling increased. Loose rocks began pelting them and the wooden bracing began to quiver. The timbers shoring up the sides and roof were different here. The braces were no longer new but gray and decayed. They splintered. Some of them came tumbling down with a waterfall of rocks.

The tunnel was caving in.

Della screamed. A deafening rumble of falling rocks and timber roared through the passage like a racing locomotive coming up behind them.

Colin pushed her ahead of him. "Run!"

She spurted forward but the ground was suddenly so uneven that she stumbled and barely caught herself before she hit the ground. Clouds of rising dust filled her mouth and nostrils. She couldn't see through the swirling dark haze.

"Keep going!" Colin sent her staggering forward.

She didn't see the faint light ahead until she was almost upon it. With a strangled sob of relief, she lunged toward the opening. Just as she reached it, the earth gave way behind her and an explosive burst of air sent rocks piling down upon her. She gave a choked cry as she crumpled under the weight of dirt and debris.

*   *   *

Silence. No light. Only suspended darkness. No thoughts went through her head. No emotions filled her chest. She couldn't move and felt no pain.

"My God, how long has she been here?"
"She's still breathing."
"Call an ambulance."
The voices were nebulous. She wanted to speak when someone moved the weight off her crumpled body but she couldn't. From far away she heard a piercing shrill siren. Her heavy eyelids fluttered upward. A flood of bright lights stabbed and tormented her until she gratefully floated away into a murky darkness. The pain seemed to come all at once. All over her body. She retreated from it. She let herself drift farther and farther away.

A fatherly voice kept badgering her. "Della...don't give up. You're a lucky woman. You could have been killed when that tunnel caved in."

Tunnel? Cave-in? She remembered then. Colin's hand on her back, urging her forward. She had made it to the opening just as the passage collapsed behind her. Sobs racked her body. Colin! Colin!

I'm here.

She felt his presence, an ethereal figure standing at the foot of her bed looking down at her. His dark hair and handsome face were clear but the rest of him was framed in soft white. She wanted to reach out to him but her arms were to heavy to lift. Her vision blurred in a wash of sharp pain. When she opened her eyes again, he was gone.

No, no. Don't leave me. Take me with you.

"You have to fight, Della," the professional-sounding voice insisted. "You're a young woman. You have a whole lifetime ahead of you."

A lifetime? An eternity without Colin? She lay awake in the darkness. *He was waiting for her.* She felt it. Somehow, she had to go to him.

"Colin . . . Colin," she whispered hoarsely.

"I'm here, love."

She slowly turned her head. A misty shadow lifted and her vision cleared. Every line and plane of his beloved face was sharp and crisp. His arm was cradled in a white sling and he was standing in front of a white curtain that had been drawn around the bed.

He bent over and kissed her with soft, tender lips. His warm breath touched her face. His blue eyes shone with joy and relief. "Welcome back."

She tried to work her mouth but no words would come. Tears flowed wetly down her cheeks. He took her hand and squeezed it. The remembered warmth of his body sluiced through her. She closed her eyes and then opened them again. He was still there.

"Are we . . . dead?" she whispered weakly.

He chuckled lightly and brushed back moist hair from her forehead. "No, love. We're very much alive. But you had us all scared for a while. I've been here every day waiting...not knowing if you were going to make it."

No one would ever know how close she had come to giving up. She had thought that he was a ghostly figure standing by her bed. But he was alive!

He raised her hand to his mouth and kissed it tenderly. "I escaped in better shape than you did. By some miracle, I was caught in a pocket when the tunnel fell in and the entrance was blocked. I yelled and pounded but nobody heard me. It took me nearly ten hours to dig out with my one good arm. By that time, some of the workmen had found you and taken you to the hospital.''

''And everything's the same . . . as when we left?''

He shook his head. ''My life will never be the same. No more dark doubts. No specters from the past haunting me. I'm free to make of life what I will. And if you'll marry me, I pledge to love and cherish you with every breath I draw.''

''In every lifetime?'' she questioned with a teasing smile.

''Every single one,'' he promised and kissed her passionately to prove it.

A white-haired, beaming doctor came in the room. ''Well, well, look at what we have here. A pretty young lady kissing the guy who's been camping out in this room for three weeks.''

Days, weeks or eternity? Della looked into Colin's engulfing eyes. She had learned that time could not be contained in earthly measurements. Some existences were timeless.

''You had a nasty concussion but I'm glad to say that the swelling is going down nicely. You'll be good as new.'' The doctor gave them a fatherly frown. ''But I'd stay out of old tunnels from now on if I were you.''

Colin exchanged a knowing smile with Della. ''You have our word on it.''

*   *   *   *   *

COMING NEXT MONTH

#667 HER SECRET, HIS CHILD—Paula Detmer Riggs
Intimate Moments Extra

For sixteen years Carly Alderson had lived with a secret, embodied by her daughter. Yet Carly had never dreamed the past would catch up with her, or that Mitch Scanlon would remember.... He'd changed her life one long-ago night—and now held her very future in his hands.

#668 HIDING JESSICA—Alicia Scott
Romantic Traditions/The Guiness Gang

Mitch Guiness knew how to re-create a person from head to toe, but Jessica Gavornee was one tough lady to change. A federally protected witness, she refused to trust Mitch with her innermost fears—and secrets—allowing him access that went only skin-deep. But Mitch found himself wanting much more....

#669 UNDERCOVER MAN—Merline Lovelace
Code Name: Danger

Sweet, demure Paige Lawrence's engagement had gone bust. Though David Jensen still owned her heart, she sensed that he had other things on his mind. Then she learned the truth behind his lies—and found herself risking everything for her undercover lover.

#670 DEFENDING HIS OWN—Beverly Barton
The Protectors

He was the best. Deborah Vaughn knew there were worse things than being guarded by Ashe McLaughlin. Getting killed, to name just one. But she couldn't shake her response to his remembered touch—or the fear that he would discover their child born of deception....

#671 OUR CHILD?—Sally Tyler Hayes

Ten years ago her sister's kidnapping had wrenched Carolyn McKay and Drew Delaney apart. Now Drew had returned, a missing-children expert intent on breaking that case and a new one with frightening similarities. But Carolyn wondered if Drew could handle reopening the past...and finding the child he never knew he had.

#672 ONE FORGOTTEN NIGHT—Suzanne Sanders
Premiere

Detective Mike Novalis had sworn never to compromise himself again. He'd been burned once by a beautiful prime suspect, and he feared Nina Dennison was no different. But Nina remembered nothing of her past—let alone whether she was guilty or innocent. And the only man she trusted was the one she should have feared most.

Take 4 bestselling love stories FREE

Plus get a FREE surprise gift!

Tall, dark and...dangerous...

Strangers in the Night

Just in time for the exciting Halloween season, Silhouette brings you three spooky love stories in this fabulous collection. You will love these original stories that combine sensual romance with just a taste of danger. Brought to you by these fabulous authors:

Anne Stuart

Chelsea Quinn Yarbro

Maggie Shayne

Available in October at a store near you.

Only from

Silhouette®

—where passion lives.

Five unforgettable couples say "I Do"... with a little help from their friends!

Always a Bridesmaid!

Silhouette Shadows presents
THE ABANDONED BRIDE
by Jane Toombs...
book four of Always a Bridesmaid!–
Silhouette's five-book series about the lives,
loves–and weddings–of five couples in Clover,
South Carolina.

As Lucy Maguire and her fiancé are about to
exchange vows, a mysterious man bursts into the
church–and the groom-to-be runs away faster
than you can say "I Do!" Max Ryder sure knows
how to make an entrance into a lady's life....

Don't miss Lucy and Max's story when
Always a Bridesmaid! continues with
THE ABANDONED BRIDE (chock-full
of big surprises!) by Jane Toombs, available in
September...only from Silhouette Shadows.

V *Silhouette*®
TM

AAB-4

Become a
Privileged Woman,
You'll be entitled to all
these Free Benefits.
And Free Gifts, too.

To thank you for buying our books, we've designed an exclusive FREE program called *PAGES & PRIVILEGES™*. You can enroll with just one Proof of Purchase, and get the kind of luxuries that, until now, you could only read about.

BIG HOTEL DISCOUNTS

A privileged woman stays in the finest hotels. And so can you—at up to 60% off! Imagine standing in a hotel check-in line and watching as the guest in front of you pays $150 for the same room that's only costing you $60. Your *Pages & Privileges* discounts are good at Sheraton, Marriott, Best Western, Hyatt and thousands of other fine hotels all over the U.S., Canada and Europe.

FREE DISCOUNT TRAVEL SERVICE

A privileged woman is always jetting to romantic places.

When <u>you</u> fly, just make one phone call for the lowest published airfare at time of booking— or double the difference back!

PLUS—you'll get a $25 voucher to use the first time you book a flight AND <u>5% cash back on every ticket you buy thereafter through the travel service!</u>